Intermission

Owen Martell grew up in Pontneddfechan, South Wales. He has published two previous novels in Welsh, and has won the Wales Book of the Year Award.

Praise for *Intermission*

'An introspective, original novel . . . It is hard to write about figures of recent history in a way that feels authentic and true, but Bill Evans is drawn here in all his quirkiness and mutability . . . This novel stands as a well-written lament. It is a clear-eyed exploration of a jazz intermission, of the forced break in the chaos, and an apt tribute to a music so full of life that even a pause, a silence, can go down howling.'

Guardian

'This fine if elusive novel about a jazz giant echoes his art in both its style and its story-telling . . . A novel as oblique, elusive but quietly hypnotic as its hero's own playing . . . This domestic suite in its entirety pays homage to Evans's art of elliptical refinement. Through discontinuous moods, modes and moments we both get to know the family and, indirectly, touch the roots of Bill's own gift . . . *Intermission* might prove simply too rarefied and intangible for some tastes; too disdainful of the sweet chords and easy resolutions of major-key story-telling . . . Yet the suite – as in another collage-style quest for a jazz legend, Michael Ondaatje's Buddy Bolden novel *Coming through Slaughter* – follows an inner logic of its own.'

Independent

'A vivid depiction of the 1960s New York music scene, it has a wonderfully noirish feel – and scoops our prize for best cover design.'

Elle Decoration

Intermission

Owen Martell

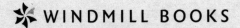
WINDMILL BOOKS

Published by Windmill Books 2014

2 4 6 8 10 9 7 5 3 1

First published in Great Britain in 2013 by William Heinemann

Windmill Books
The Random House Group Limited
20 Vauxhall Bridge Road, London SW1V 2SA

Addresses for companies within The Random House Group Limited
can be found at: www.randomhouse.co.uk/offices.htm

The Random House Group Limited Reg. No. 954009

www.randomhouse.co.uk

A CIP catalogue record for this book
is available from the British Library

ISBN 9780099558828

The Random House Group Limited supports the Forest Stewardship
Council® (FSC®), the leading international forest-certification organisation.
Our books carrying the FSC label are printed on FSC®-certified paper. FSC is
the only forest-certification scheme supported by the leading environmental
organisations, including Greenpeace. Our paper procurement policy can be
found at: www.randomhouse.co.uk/environment

Typeset in Adobe Caslon (11/16pt) by
Palimpsest Book Production Limited, Falkirk, Stirlingshire
Printed and bound by CPI Group (UK) Ltd, Croydon, CR0 4YY

i Twm
ac i'm rhieni

CONTENTS

Don't play what's there, play what's not there.

Miles Davis

INTERMISSION

THE PETRUSHKA CHORD
[HARRY]

IMPROMPTU

It was late in the evening, after dinner and Debby, before Harry got a chance to open the paper. Nearly two whole days had passed since the accident, which he read about now full of grim excitement. A prickly heat raced through him. The report was short – more news in brief than news itself – but the sadness of the circumstances, and the notion that the circles of loss might yet extend beyond the immediate upstate vicinity, had ensured its newsworthiness. It even mentioned his brother – and the heat came to finger-like points beneath his skin. Mr LaFaro, it said, was to be seen recently performing with the Bill Evans Trio at the Village Vanguard club in Greenwich Village.

Harry had seen the deceased, met him, almost spoken to him. They went down for the afternoon set on Sunday, Pat and Debby and him. Bill introduced them after they'd finished. Scotty, I'd like you to meet my brother Harry. Hi Harry. Hi Scotty, he'd wanted to say back, you were great, before contenting himself with nodding and grasping the young man's hand.

Scotty handled his bass with implausible, almost arrogant ease. The arrogant part of it wasn't directed at the instrument itself though, nor even at the listening audience. It was more a comfortable disregard for all that he might have played, that which fell away definitively as soon as he'd placed firm-sliding fingers where he'd always meant them to be. If Harry wasn't able to hear him improvising, on a June afternoon, it was because improvising wasn't the word. He was doing something else, something that wasn't even audible in Bill's playing.

And now he was dead. Harry thought of the fingers he'd seen and felt, thwanging and plucking, roughly affectionate on the neck of his bass like a farmer's handling livestock. When he took them in his own hand, they seemed quite unshakeable. He thought of them on the steering wheel then, in the instants before the crash, their grip loosening in increments of equal fatality as his concentration, the way he'd seemed to assert his being by always being *on*, lapsed at last. He wondered if he had family, a wife, children, and thought of Debby, asleep in the next room, the way her fingers used to retain the shape – the absence – of his index finger, long after she'd fallen asleep and he'd got up, as if to leave the room, but unable still to take his eyes off her. And he thought of Bill, meek and reedy. He felt afraid for him, suddenly.

Harry folded the paper and put it down next to him, on the empty place on the sofa. Pat was in the kitchen washing the dishes from dinner and he seemed to hear a spongy layer of soap cushioning the impact as she placed them on the draining board.

He got to his feet and went over to the little telephone table in the corner of the room. He lifted the receiver and dialled Bill's number. He took the base of the telephone in his hand and stood facing the window. There was a fleeting reflection of their father in the glass. Putting the receiver to his ear, he felt a twitching in his own fingers. He let the phone on the other side ring for a good half a minute or so, wondering how long it might have been before he found out had he not seen the paper. There was no answer.

§

He put the phone down and went into the kitchen, stood next to his wife and picked up a tea towel and a plate from the draining board. He played over in his mind the twenty seconds of his encounter with Scott. You remember that bassist we saw, playing with Bill? He died. He was in a car accident. Harry put the plate back, unwiped. That was probably twenty seconds right there. Pat looked up at him.

He tried Bill's phone again and, getting no answer, went to get his shoes from the hallway. In two minutes flat, he was down on the street.

§

Nearly ten o'clock but still light. Coming off the steps that led down to the pavement, he caught the falling sun full and shut his eyes briefly. He opened them again onto the pavement itself and set about walking, an insistence in his shoulders, as if the effort he put in now would be totted up later for possible gains. When he got to the end of the block he changed into a higher gear and crossed the street, in time with the gathering chorus of engines waiting for the lights to change. He headed downtown, towards the subway station, and the first hints of a night breeze, blowing up off the Hudson, came upon him. Exhaust fumes too, flecked with copper. The breeze caught a lock of his hair, those loose strands that decided every morning which side of his parting they'd register their allegiance to. They were flicking back and forth, in agitation, and he tried repeatedly to smooth them down, even licking his palm.

He walked again through the meeting with Scott, thinking of Bill's part in it this time, so as to be better prepared for what was awaiting him.

He'd wanted to introduce them, Harry thought. It wasn't done for form's sake or out of some obligation, familial or other. There had been plenty of other gigs when he'd barely got a word out of his brother afterwards, let alone mumbled introductions. So it was either that Bill liked Scott's playing particularly and envisaged a lasting partnership, or that he liked him personally. Either way, he'd thought it worth introducing them. More likely was that it was both – an opposite identicality of their playing together; traits and tics, habits and modes that found each other on the bandstand, where it didn't particularly matter if one was vigorous and athletic, for example, the other anything but now, so long as they came, by whatever means, to the murmured accord. And now one of them was dead.

You wouldn't have put them together, that was for sure. Scott was happy to assume all the authority of his youth. Bill, thirty-two in August but only a few years older, looked like the junior partner. You'd have said, coming at them blind, that they were too different. Scott was astounding – he actually sounded as good as he looked. Bill, on the other hand, well, you heard him feeling his way. Or you felt him listening. You saw, in any case, the way it troubled him – in the sense of movement inside, rather than affliction necessarily – the way he bent double over the piano, head almost touching the keys, fingers like willow stalks dragging along in the swell.

Then you spoke to him after the gig and he wanted to fade into the decor. As if the places he played weren't already dimly lit or unfussy enough. He didn't want to talk about the set or listen to you tell him that you'd enjoyed it. There wasn't even any of the passive arrogance, the way you couldn't help but look as if you were abashed *and* feigning abashment when you came off stage and people said nice things.

§

In the subway, looking into the tunnel as he waited for the first light of his approaching train, he thought of the Holland Tunnel, opened the year of his birth, and the way everything on the other side belonged to Jersey and to childhood. The first time he saw Manhattan from the turnpike. A long, guileful crocodile, idling in the Hudson, the towers of midtown its beady eyes. Bus rides.

He took Pat and Debby out there shortly after they'd set up in New York. It was late summer and the houses where they'd lived, Bill and him and Harry Sr and Mary, seemed impossibly green and growing when they compared them, the three of them together, encouraging Debby to list the places *she* could remember living, to the cramping necessity of their new place in the city. There was a ceramic swan outside the house on Hunter Avenue and a new car too. The house itself had been given new windows.

They stayed into early evening and the sun disappeared behind the trees just as it always had. The change in the light announced, or so it had always seemed to Harry, the arrival of the trains, even to the point of enabling you to hear them at last; the distant wailing, a call not only of their vast American continent but of oceans too, whale song, marbled and blue.

Bill was everywhere that afternoon – on trees they'd climbed, in upstairs windows and in the air itself, where the footballs seemed to fly still, from the bottom end of the garden, where there was no fence to separate their patch from the street, all the way up to the little ridge outside the kitchen window, back when he played quarterback, when he had cheeks, and arms and legs that didn't look like they'd snap in two at the first remotely bruising contact.

§

Harry was met by hot gusting wind when he came up the stairs at 86th Street. With every step as he walked down Broadway, he felt his shirt sopping cold against the small of his back. The heat seemed to hit him in waves, yielding the day's accumulation slowly, like a poisoner dosing his victims. Ground heat, seepage from the paving stones and buildings, from telephone kiosks and rubbish bins piled high and wide on street corners. Emanating also from the entire subway network beneath his feet, geothermal portent of a swelter deeper still. Everywhere was heat, he thought; the whole city. Every body.

He slowed his pace but, unwilling to let his guard down entirely, tried at the same time to prick up his senses, as though expecting to run into his brother not just around any corner but around all of them. He wanted to prepare himself for meeting Bill but felt himself bothered by the notion of there being any need to; the fact that his turning up unannounced would be registered by both of them in precisely those terms. He'd allowed himself to imagine that living in the same place as his brother – for the first time since they'd left New Jersey – would be governed by their previous knowledge of each other. The old rules had lapsed, however. Those of their parents lingered, albeit severely weakened by the fifteen-year hiatus – but they'd never been absolute anyway. Bill and he hadn't ever dropped in except on each other's bedrooms and had to ask now whether the other took sugar in his coffee.

When he tried to think of the right thing to say when he saw him, Harry found himself imagining instead ways in which he might speak of Bill to strangers who'd come asking. He'd insist, he thought, in the first place, on the inalienability of the past, how he was there, in everything, to try and mask the fact that there were other people who, in the day-to-day sense at least, knew him better now. But he'd be taken in, he thought, like plenty of others besides, by Bill's growing celebrity. A handful of albums already and polls in *Billboard* and *DownBeat* that had him coming to the top of his game. People might coax him into accepting a part in that too. They'd associate the two of them, increasingly, by their common name. I don't suppose you're related to *Bill* Evans, laughing. He's my brother, he'd say, and agree as he did so to the terms they were offering. Then they'd respond either enthusiastically, at which point, he knew, he'd want to give them back untouched the quickly taken glory, or else with indifference, to all of it *en somme* – the dollar gigs in Catskill Mountain resorts, meals at the kitchen table, the whole New Jersey scrapbook – as if their connection to Bill went beyond his. He's *my* brother, he'd want to say then, before thinking finally that it would be all he wanted, in fact, for Bill to be just as unknown as he'd ever been, untethered with genius, the old couplings holding firm. That way he'd be able to say, He's just my brother – and get away with telling them nothing.

§

Arriving at last at West 83rd, Harry turned towards the park. It was sufficiently dark for men in doorways to appear only as he came up alongside them and he felt their eyes upon him for five paces or so when he'd gone by. In one doorway, he saw a man curled against the stone steps with what looked like a balled-up pair of socks in his mouth. At the wide front door to Bill's building, he rang the buzzer.

There was no answer and he rang again, two or three insistent bursts in quick succession, as if to try and rouse him, and rouse himself from an image of his brother stricken that was trying to take hold in his mind.

He wasn't in – but there was no great mystery. He was with friends, maybe, or at a gig, that was all. He'd still have to work. He couldn't just stop working. It was what he did, what he was, and there'd be times when he had to play even when he didn't particularly feel like it.

Back home, Harry thought, back to wife and child.

Before starting the walk to the subway, he looked up the street, as if to prove to anybody looking down on them that he was going about his brotherly task with rigour. It was then that he saw Bill, walking through the domed glow of a streetlight – like a drooping flower, even the built world coming out in sympathy tonight – some forty or fifty yards away, heading towards the park.

Tall, slightly buckled frame, hands thrust hard into the pockets of his jacket, as if he wanted to push the rest of himself into their protection too. Harry was about to call out but decided against it at the last moment. He ran out onto the pavement, though, and started after him briskly.

When he got to the end of the block, Bill crossed over to the park side of the street, turning left, uptown. He was walking close by the perimeter wall, out of reach of the lights now. And he'd only just left, which meant that he'd known a visit was imminent. In all along, Harry thought, and he let the phrase intone in his mind laced with annoyance and disappointment.

§

Bill kept walking and Harry followed ten yards or so behind, like the lover rejected who can't give up the object of his ardour. Block after block, counting up the numbers, in rapid succession suddenly. Bill's gait was just long enough to keep him keen. And the more they walked like that, Bill apparently unaware of his being followed, the more Harry found himself wanting to help him. Particularly if Bill's business was in Harlem. He wouldn't be able to do much, in all probability, beyond bear silent witness, but at least he'd be looking out for him, like he'd looked out for him before, the heedful older brother. Behind the scenes, not for the gratitude, but for the good-deededness of it. It would make their mother happy too, he thought, and he had a little laugh to himself. Not that she'd know the half of it.

§

When they got into the 90s, Bill seemed to hesitate. He slowed his pace briefly before picking it up again. A little while later, in the 100s, nearing the corner of the park and directly under a streetlight again, he stopped abruptly. Before Harry had a chance to react, Bill had turned on his heel to face him head-on, albeit at the same ten-yard remove.

How could he possibly have known Harry was there? He hadn't once looked back or cast even a glance over his shoulder all the time they'd been walking. And, knowing, how could he possibly not have said anything?

They seemed to stare at each other for a few seconds and Bill even took a few steps towards Harry. But the expression on his face, Harry saw now, was of such blank unknowing that there was no way he could have seen him. The immediate impression had less to do with Bill himself than with an image of them from above, like the one Harry'd had on the doorstep – only that the observing being was more vigilant this time. And a judgement too: how perfectly strange that we should come to this, here. He was back down at street level quickly enough and tried to conduct a quick all-over survey of his brother before him.

Bill didn't look particularly good, that was certain, but that had been the case for a fair while already and the gauntness of his features, even in the paleful light, struck Harry with less force than it had when he'd seen him for the first time in New York. Then it was like looking at something cadaverous, eaten. He thought of pictures they'd had taken, at eight or nine and ten or eleven years old respectively. Individual formal portraits of them both, Mary dragging them out to Dunellen early one Saturday morning. Bill had his violin under his right arm and, behind gold-rimmed glasses, one big eye that already seemed to be staring down the years. It was that image that held sway, like something had since disappeared from his eyes, like he'd spent the intervening years unmaking, even to the point of reproach, the brilliant child.

The oddest thing about Bill now was his clothes. His trousers seemed to be a good two sizes too big for him and his shirt was billowing, as much as it could under the ever-present corduroy jacket. Nothing about him billowed as a rule. He was an odd-looking brother, Harry thought. He might even have said, if it wasn't so preposterous, that the clothes he had on weren't his.

Lifting his head, so that his gaze was unmistakeably on Harry, but still as unseeing as before, Bill brought his right hand up to his face and, for two seconds or so, held his earlobe between thumb and forefinger. Whether it was an itch or a gesture not otherwise related to his conscious being was hard to tell. Then, clicking into gear again as abruptly as he'd stopped, he set off across the road to Harry's left, as if to go back, on the other side of the avenue, the way they'd just come.

Harry let him get to the other side before setting off after him. Where the hell was he going?

§

They went west and, between the park and the subway station at 103rd, under the influence of Bill's radiating silence, Harry tried to think things through calmly. But they were brothers, and they were walking in a city of however many millions and getting no closer to each other than stray dogs. He thought of families he'd heard of, siblings who shared the same room for years on end and never spoke, arguments that started off small, manifesting themselves in daily tests of will until, before you knew it, half a lifetime had gone by. Arguments about money, the way you brought up children. He felt afraid, like he might fall into Bill's pull, like everything around him was churning unrest.

He recalled his determination of a half-hour previous,

though, and decided to see him to his destination before going back home. Pat would be wondering where he'd got to. Bill didn't look as bad as he might. If nothing else, he was functioning. He was up and about, getting on with things – and Harry let himself be persuaded. It was only to be expected, he thought, recalling the rejection he'd felt at seeing his brother flee, that he wouldn't want to see too many people right now or that he'd prefer to choose his audiences carefully. He probably had plenty of practical stuff to think about besides. Band things, bookings. Enough to keep him from going under anyway, which was good. He'd come around in his own time.

Harry felt relief, all the agitation he'd channelled since picking up the newspaper draining away, as though to merge with the river through gulches under his feet. They walked on.

§

At the subway station, he arrived just in time to see the last of Bill's going underground. The disappearance brought with it the urgent need to go after him and Harry launched himself down the steps. He barged his way through the gate and, in a mid-step freeze, opted for the downtown branch. He'd guessed right and caught sight of Bill at the far end of the platform just as the train was pulling in. Sustained metal shrieking and cries too, of joy and aggravation, rolling around the walls.

§

At every station, Harry leapt to the carriage doors to scan the platform. He did so as discreetly as he could, as conscious of appearing odd in the eyes of the other passengers as he was afraid of being sprung. Bill was still on the train, a few carriages down.

He wasn't to be woken from his sleepwalk, Harry decided. Let him wander the dream city unimpeded, unknown to all except his visions.

They came up for air, a midsummer midnight, in the Village, and Harry knew then where Bill was going. He watched him walk up 7th Avenue, towards the propped-up awning and purple effacing neon. He heard music – rolling toms peppered with Max Roach kicks and a saxophone back in the mix, working hard to keep up. Poor souls, he thought, these jazzmen, called to tunes they could play but couldn't hum.

As Bill went out of view finally, Harry tried to tell himself that he wasn't meant to have seen him that evening. The feeling all the same was that he'd abandoned his brother, along with all responsibility for him. And not only to the night; he'd given him over to strangers whose touch he'd have to depend upon now for intimations of home. He imagined a scene. No one would notice Bill coming in and he'd sit at the bar and listen without ears to whoever was playing. Eventually, somebody – a barman, maybe, someone who knew him by sight – would see him sitting there and they'd come around, from behind the bar, to place a hand on his shoulder, squeezingly.

PRELUDE FOR SIX HANDS

The first trio was with Mary, at home. They'd get back from school, Bill and he, to the accompaniment of her piano. Her playing would be audible through the walls from fully thirty yards away, the notes snaking their way through the air like cartoon aromas. They'd break into a gallop and race each other to the front door, trying to outrun the feeling – they sensed it in each other, it made them squeal and run even faster – that they were being chased, like they were spooked cattle.

When they got into the house, though, having already untangled their arms from their coats, there was Mary waiting for them.

She'd be at the piano in the living room, sitting die-straight on the stool, which she'd covered in avocado green as soon as Bill started school and she had at least some time to herself again. She seemed to inhabit the space around the instrument better, more comfortably, than any other in the house. In the kitchen, for example, when she set down the evening meal on chipped plates before them, she was grudgingly efficient; when they sat in the living room after dinner, resolutely American, at Harry Sr's behest, and felt the heat pouring off him like he was a busted valve, she seemed to take everything upon herself, too weary by then for protest.

At the piano, though, she hammered out such strident, rollicking lines that the old upright, bought for how much was it from a man clearing out his dead mother's house, seemed to be doing all it could not to fall apart like one of Chico's. She sang too to her own accompaniment, in Russian, and she allowed the boys to join in on these occasions. She never taught them the words, nor any Russian come to that, so they sang the sounds, as if they had their mouths full of yoghurt. They loved it. The drama, the despair, the those-were-the-days of it they seemed to know instinctively. It made them think in turn – made *Harry* think – of their grandmother, when she came to meet them at the front door. Her greetings were always a gurgling stream of affective, effusive Os, muddied Es, and Rs which broke the surface like coarse bedload. English be damned. She'd haul them into her embrace, ruffling their hair on her bosom, while Mary, tutting, looked on.

§

Harry seemed to enjoy the singing more than his brother. It was something instinctive, perhaps – you were always a choir when you sang, never entirely alone. Or else it was the firstborn in him; never more his father's son and namesake than when he gave himself over to the same pious abandon he'd already seen acted out before him a hundred times – father and friends, men of a certain age and uncertain standing who got together every so often to down whiskey and hymns. He clicked his heels together, held up his chin and sang to the unknown ancestor, hanging as if by his black moustache and white starched collar above the piano.

By the time they got to the end of the second verse, tired of approximating the words, he'd have edged towards the piano. Always to his mother's left, he followed the jumping bass of her left hand with his right, a quarter of a beat late. He favoured correctness, even of the laboured kind, over imprudence, but he was quick enough to catch on and he held her back only rarely.

Bill too caught on quickly enough. He started off copying a copy – going to the piano after Harry's lessons to try and reproduce, trying their father's patience into the bargain, what he'd heard from his position on the sofa. He brought this prodding to their trio. He was less certain of himself, of what it was he was meant to be playing – but even then perhaps he was better equipped to follow. And he would

have found also increasingly – wouldn't he? How might it
have been? – that he could actually teach himself: not to
hear the wrong notes he played, tune out the clumsy
fingering and concentrate instead on the unfolding glory.
It happens in me, not in the wood, not in the strings. So
that when finally he started having lessons of his own,
making up the deficit in big bear bounds, he'd already have
delegated what was essential from his young mind to his
fingers.

Harry wondered how happy they might have looked – if
they would actually have looked happy, that is – if he were
able to go back into the living room in Hunter Avenue and
see the three of them playing together like that. The very
first trio in which, to Mary's stern, approving nods, Bill's
mistakes became flourishes.

§

How young they were, Harry thought, how ordinary. That
they should have become adults, gone off to the army, met
women and had children, or that Bill, by all accounts, took
heroin now, seemed not just inconceivable but impossible.
It was as if they'd tried to pencil in credible adult moustaches
on their school photos. How ordinary their surroundings
were, their parents' ambitions – for themselves and for their
children too. Mary only wanted some vague best for them,

Harry Sr's American dreaming was paper-thin and green. What part had love ever played in their lives, Harry Jr wondered, love like he felt for Debby – a love that got no easier to bear, in the sense that time might conceivably have rendered it ordinary too, and which seemed to grow exponentially, encompassing all she'd been and could have been, all she was and might yet be, until it was a quantum agglomeration in which his love was the constant not because she was his daughter and he'd love her regardless but because it came about the same in every iteration. *That* was something extraordinary, he thought, and he felt a sapping in his body, like he'd been tapped at the knees; premonition of a time when he might no longer have the necessary processing power.

§

On Hunter Avenue, then later when they moved to Greenbrook Road, it sometimes happened that they walked together-apart like they'd walk up Central Park West, what was it, twenty-odd years later. Their trio had petered out by then; too old suddenly to sing songs they didn't understand and less enamoured of not understanding. Too knowing, precisely, and too involved with the world outside their cloister to play along. They were both quite the young musicians by then in any case. Still perfectly ordinary, though, still nothing – outwardly at least, apart from the handmade bills and posters advertising gigs they imagined putting on – to distinguish either of them from the competition in Central Jersey.

Back then, it was Harry who led the way with Bill following a few yards behind him, far enough away to avoid the accusations of clinging to his older brother – cheating the schoolboy code – but close enough all the same to benefit from his support should the need arise. Harry felt himself bolstered, he remembered, by his position of strength, the offering of sibling fealty. You knew you were older but it was a straight fight all the same. Bill seemed happy enough with the arrangement. The older boys' attentions – name-calling, the occasional confiscation of his school bag – were unwelcome, but they were bearable too, not to say acceptable. That is, whereas he would no doubt have preferred to do without them, as it was he seemed to take things upon himself – Mary bis but without the attendant sense of injustice. You might even have said, serious-minded in a way that only children could be, that he already regarded the intrusion as necessary in some way, a sort of training.

Either way, the pattern seemed to be established, the eye above regarding them as they regarded themselves: in this incarnation they'd follow each other, compulsively.

Later, they went to Dunellen for their piano lessons,

bombing down on their bikes in hot pursuit, taking each other's slipstream and getting as low down on the rickety frames as they dared. They followed one another into Mrs Leland's house for Harry to have his lesson first so long as Bill's came immediately after.

They waited alone for the other to finish. When Harry came into the room, Bill was always sitting stock still in one of the armchairs, looking at the wall. He might well have been running about the place, crazed and hot, and have returned to the chair just in time for the door to open, but it always looked like he'd been sitting there like that the whole time.

During his empty half-hour, Harry concentrated occasionally on the broken tonk of Bill's lesson through the wall and pottered about the room, picking things up and putting them down again. The space had a particular effect on him and he'd often thought of the bare walls and threadbare chairs since, one unknowing day, he'd seen them for the last time. Mrs Leland called it the living room but Harry couldn't imagine anyone actually using it as such. Beyond the form and larger fixtures, he remembered specific items which reeled out bleakly in his mind: the little table, corralled with woodworm, on which he placed the glass of water they were given while they waited; a box of matches adorned with a longboat and orange sail, three burnt stubs inside; an abridged copy of *Huck Finn*, provided specifically, it seemed, since there were no other books in the room, for the children who came to the house. Harry spent most of the time looking out of the window.

When he did so, however, gazing down from his first-floor vantage onto the street below, even the view seemed to suck up into the room. Funnelled by the bay window, his consciousness itself took on the blank dimensions. He saw men like his father congregating outside the bar, women like his mother carrying bags of groceries, children like him, but more like Bill in fact, running around or riding their bikes. They gathered in the back of his mind, distant and untouchable. That he might yet go down there and be just like them seemed not to occur to him.

He'd turn back into the room then to consider, and from his adult position now too, the absoluteness of parents' houses, as if they were the perfect critique of the life you lived elsewhere. Living rooms weren't as comfortable, as lived in, precisely, as they were where the sofas already bore the imprint not only of your own legs and backside but of others similarly endowed – your own particular familial podge. But it wasn't even the physical space as such, or not only, anyway, nor the furniture, nor even the word 'home'. It was the space it occupied in your mind, rather, your constructing mind. And then those rooms became their own perfect critique because they weren't yours any more, if ever they had been. It made him think of the dreams he'd had – actual dreams as well as figures of speech – and which he still had from time to time. I want this, he'd tell himself, dressed in a purple jumpsuit, parading on an open-top bus, and again when he took Pat and Debby up to see his parents at Christmas, this but mine.

§

On weekends, it was over to their cousins, where Harry Sr paraded them before his wife's family, and insisted squarely on them being *his* boys. Listen to this, he'd say, *listen*, when the assembled gathering hushed respectfully *but not respectfully enough* for their recitals. Harry first, eldest and still best for the time being, then Bill. Their father compered them enthusiastically. You thought that was good, he'd say, now listen to Bill, he's only eight or nine or ten or eleven, as though prodigy were no more than a question of being younger than somebody else.

§

Then, one day, they were playing outside in the garden when Bill fell out of a tree and broke his wrist. Harry saw the fall. They were trying to get as high as they could in the knotted birch, urging each other on, though Bill's movements, he could tell, had become suddenly tense and guarded. Harry saw the flow of negative energy – a displacement of colour by its absence – from Bill's eyes, through his neck and into his arms and fingers. He plummeted and landed on the grass with a dead welt. There was a whole two seconds of silence as Bill laid wilfully still. When he cried out at last his pain was given added voice by a perfectly timed freight train tearing through early evening.

Harry climbed down as fast as he could and, not even stopping to look at his stricken brother, ran towards the house. He got there just as Mary was opening the back door and bringing her hand up to her mouth. He ran into her and, to stop himself without falling and out of fear too, or guilt, threw his arms around her waist. She ran her hands through his hair quite calmly, he remembered, for a few seconds, until she came to, not screaming but gasping.

She went into overdrive in the weeks that followed. Bill was kept to his room, as though his condition was chronic, and Mary bought him records and scores and even took the record player upstairs. She didn't play the piano either and, with Bill unable to, it was as if they'd decided between them that if he couldn't play, nobody should. Harry had the living room entirely to himself when he practised and they arrived home from school now to piped dances and polkas, Debussy, Stravinsky, *Petrushka*.

Bill came into the living room one afternoon while Harry was at the piano. He stood quietly at the bass end, looking into the space between the end of his brother's fingers and the keys. He moved after a while to stand behind Harry's left shoulder. Harry stopped playing immediately and turned around accusingly. But Bill didn't say a word. Harry made certain of registering his complaint before going back to his playing. He was sufficiently put out, though, as if he'd been aware of a pretence at play, that he blustered his way through the rest of his practice with clodded fingers.

When Bill's wrist was more or less properly mended, they reformed their trio – for one night only, as it were. They came home together – had they both started high school? – to the sound of Mary's piano. She was banging out a Shrovetide dance and the notes, snaking their way on the breeze, were odorous like before and evocative but, curiously, not of anything lived. When they got into the house they took up their previous positions either side of her and played along, much improved, flourishing.

THEME

Harry woke up in the morning heavy with duty. The bedroom he shared with his wife was full of it, even the walls coated with a translucent veneer that seemed, while he was awake but not to the material world, to be a barrier between him and another realm more obliging. The shadow of a TV antenna on the wall embossed mountain-like in his mind, all ridges and fallings-away.

It was already two whole semesters since he'd brought his family up to New York and something about that formulation still gave him a jolt. The way he found himself telling it to people when they asked seemed less a recounting of events than a call to manly action. *His* family, following *his* lead. Throughout the academic year, all the implied responsibility of fatherhood – the first sixteen or so years of more or less total dependence, followed by long years in which he'd contribute silently, passively, though no less significantly perhaps, to Debby's welfare – had settled in him deeper even than when she was newborn. And this had coupled with a modified sense of his real, day-to-day responsibilities; the way he'd uprooted her young life and plonked it down again in uncertainty. He couldn't do his thesis *and* teach full-time so he'd taken on a few private students – that had kept them going during term time, even if they'd had to dip into reserves accumulated during the early years of their married life. But then they'd always saved with Debby in mind anyway, even when it wasn't her specifically . . .

Most troublesome, perhaps, was the thought of having duties to himself, in his own right. He couldn't bring himself to contemplate not finishing at Columbia but had had to make it in his mind subsequently that what was good for him would be good for the girls too in the long run. As much as he might want to do his PhD for himself, the girls actually *required* it of him . . . Not that that made the experience of being a student again – and in New York – any less strange.

During the first couple of months, he'd tried to recall the wonderings of his boyhood: what it might feel like to be someone who lived in the city – in an apartment, taking the subway and queuing for a sandwich with actors and sportsmen. Increasingly, though, he found himself walking the 90s and into the 100s as though through a parcel of disputed land. The zone extended, in space, across from

New Jersey into uptown Manhattan and, in the nebulous realm, from Home to Life. How exactly the four ends tied together he was never sure, only that the territory itself was bisected north–south by the Hudson.

He oriented himself by the river and tried to keep in mind its lowland constance. And the affinity grew, almost to the extent that he could feel the weight in his brain tipping over into the side closest to the flow at any given moment. In the morning, when he made his way up to campus – left brain to the fore – the disputed territory was no more than a syllogistic direct line; you had to come from somewhere and his somewhere was over there. You crossed the river to get there. When he made his way back home, though, the Hudson on his right, his thoughts too seemed to have flipped. Bathed now in the coloured abstraction of city blocks that were arranged like orange groves in the setting sun and watered from the self-same Hudson. Crossing it led you inexorably home. The feeling then was of a newly pressed, juicy belonging, as though the Plainfield of his youth had been bounteous beyond.

§

Pat was already in the kitchen getting Sunday going. They'd tried to instil in Debby an idea of it being a day of rest

– to no avail. Harry heard her through the wall, stirring, getting out of bed and banging about. Then her door banged and he heard her bare footsteps in the hall. He thought of having duties forced upon him, some of which he'd accepted gladly, others he'd assumed because he wanted to be a good man. And others still rushing up on him from his youth with linebacking insistence. It never even crossed his mind any more that he might like to stay in bed for another half-hour. He recalled the start of his walk the night before, in the bromine sun, and felt his legs clingy in the sheets. From the bathroom, Debby shouted for a towel and he heard Pat going to the cupboard in the hallway to oblige.

Images from childhood, other walls around him, turning zoetropic. But the images behind the rotating cylinder were no more than projections themselves. They had little to do, Harry thought, with what they purported to represent. They were cheaply synecdochic and imbued increasingly with adult embarrassment. As though the unbreakable narrative of childhood could be scribbled on the plaster cast of a broken wrist.

He felt feeble and incapable as he got out of bed and it occurred to him that he was already preparing the same ground for his daughter, a cycle not of recrimination necessarily – that was its one redemption – but of ordinary lies which they were bound to repeat.

They sat down for breakfast together and Pat tried to talk to him about the night before. Her eyes were sympathetic, friendly and complicit. Then they noticed Debby looking at them and turned the conversation onto her.

§

When they'd finished eating, Pat took Debby out to the park and Harry called Mary, presuming, or strongly suspecting at least, that Bill wouldn't have. She answered on the second ring and, seized anew of a need not to waste time, he told her immediately about Scott LaFaro and that he was worried. Or not worried but . . . He left out the part about their citywide chase. Mary listened to him carefully and he felt that he had her undivided attention for once – or that her attention was unmitigated because he was telling her things she'd already sensed she needed to hear.

He'd sent her clippings from newspapers and magazines since he'd been in New York. He bought *DownBeat* regularly and kept an eye on listings, looking out for reviews and notices. Pictures too, once in a while. He knew that this pleased her; she'd read particular phrases back to him when he called or tell him things about Bill as if *she* was informing *him*. They never talked particularly about his fame – they couldn't seem to agree between them on a word to describe it adequately – but Harry knew that it pleased her too; it was exactly what she might have wished for, he thought, for her children, for Bill, had it been within her given range to do so.

She was delighted when Harry told her he was moving to New York. She'd read this too in terms of Bill in the first place, as if it was understood that he'd need help all along the way and that he, Harry, was doing the brotherly thing at last. And she'd done some reading of her own since the last time – or was it Bill himself who'd told her? Stravinsky, in any case, was in New York, conducting *Petrushka*. At Columbia. As if all Harry had to do was go up to him and give him Bill's number.

Mary didn't say very much initially and Harry looked down at his school bag, which he left in the living room most nights. He was thinking of getting some work done, while he had the place to himself. His mother was just warming up though.

It began, as always, with admonishments. You should look out for your brother. Or, Bill needs you, you know. It was as if she'd been conducting a different conversation in her head in the minutes before the call, one in which Harry was deliberately obtuse or neglectful or even someone or something else entirely – the very structures, rocky, sharp, abstract, upon which Bill's gentleness would be dashed. Then it was Debby, who'd be a New Yorker before you knew it and forget what it was, if she'd ever known, to be good and honest. Now, joy, it was Stravinsky who, the way Mary told it, embodied a return in glory – back the way they'd come, third class and diseased across the Atlantic, over the steppe, to an arrival at last in the unlapsed motherland. He and Bill should work together. It was perfectly obvious. She ended with another round of admonishments, but gentler now, as though she were coming over to the idea that Harry wasn't all bad, that he'd do what he could to help but needed a little push occasionally. Conciliatory enough, not to say affectionate by the end, that he wouldn't feel the need to force the receiver back into its berth.

§

He went out in the afternoon to walk around for a while on his own. West, towards the river, where he took his life in his hands crossing the Henry Hudson Parkway. He spent a few minutes contemplating the George Washington Bridge in the middle distance upstream. He tried to follow individual vehicles – trucks and some of the larger station wagons – across the span and realised after a while that he was staring. He was snapped back to attention by something falling, from the lattice-work understructure of the lower level, about halfway over. He could have sworn. A tool left behind by maintenance workers, perhaps, or something thrown out of a car window which had lodged there somehow until that moment. He heard, in any case, the metallic slap as it hit the surface of the water, like a saxophone fallen off its stand.

When he walked on and found himself, stopping to think, around Bill's neighbourhood, he tried to be surprised, like he hadn't been meaning to arrive there all along. He spent a good five minutes walking up and down alongside a basketball court where a group of young men were engaged in a match in which the playing seemed to come a distant second to the shouting. He wished vaguely that he didn't have to, that his brother could get by on his own, like *he* got by on *his* own. Knowing at the same time that he must, and would, go to him.

When he got to West 83rd, Bill buzzed him in and he drudged up the stairs, hitting every one, still hoping for a reprieve. The door was ajar when he got to the landing and he went through into the apartment with extreme caution. He tried Bill's name out loud, to see how it came off. Nervous was how. Forced and unfamiliar. Rhetorical.

The living room had only one feature – Bill's grand, which stood between them, imposing. Bill was sitting on the far side and a reflection of his head extended long and shining into the wood. Hey, Harry said. Hey. He squeezed his way around the instrument and stood before his brother, who looked up at him at last neither impassive nor imploring. Sorry, Harry said. I'm sorry.

§

He brought Bill home with him that evening. They came through the door, brothers together, and Pat looked up from the kitchen, smiling at them in such a way that even Harry had trouble picking the surprise on her face. He took Bill's things – a hastily filled brown leather holdall – into the living room where the fold-out table was already set for dinner. He went to get an extra plate and cutlery as Bill sat down on the sofa, curling his back into the cushions. The welcoming foam seemed to hunch his shoulders over even further and he looked just like he did at the piano, in concert. Harry wondered briefly about performance and life and caught the edge of the salad bowl in his elbow as Pat tried to skirt around him.

Their first meal together set the tone. Bill was with them in body but elsewhere – or else nowhere – in his mind. He didn't eat very much, didn't speak very much. Debby was pleased to see him but beyond kissing her cheek and calling her his favourite niece, he didn't have much to say to her either and she sensed quickly enough that something was up. Harry and Pat tried to coerce her into smalltalk about school but it was the holidays, she wasn't interested, and she'd already decided that she was better off keeping her own counsel. After dinner they watched television, Harry glad like never before that the device was what it was to life and death in America.

They left Bill to it then, seeing to Debby's bedtime together. Pat explained to her that Bill was sad at the moment, that his friend had died, and she reacted ably. She was sad for her uncle, she said, but both Harry and Pat saw as well how proud she was of her reaction. They looked at each other, amused and just a little unnerved.

For his part, Harry would have been glad of some of his daughter's instinctive comprehension and uncomplicating youth. But that itself was one of the ordinary lies, he thought. Her understanding was no less complex than either his or Pat's and his head tugged convulsively to one side, as if in disappointment.

Before going to bed, he spent a while sitting with Bill. He poured them a whiskey each, thinking it would be good older brother behaviour, and told him he should stay with them for a while. The words felt sticky on his tongue and Bill didn't respond. He didn't touch his whiskey either, not even to look at it. They pulled the window wide open to smoke a cigarette and the apartment flooded briefly with siren song. The wailing modulated in whole tones against tower blocks before tailing off, leaving the previously displaced noise to find its level again, a routine humming of life.

§

Harry woke up sometime in the middle of the night, boiling. He couldn't decide whether he'd actually been asleep or not and went to the window to lean out, hoping for a cooling current or a river breeze. He touched the top of his head with his palm. His parting was impeccably defined now, even the troublesome strands of hair at the crown stroked down by the pillow and fixed in place by sweat. He must have been asleep. He heard Pat turning onto her side and, afraid he might wake her, went back to bed.

But it wasn't Pat stirring. It was a dampened shuffling coming under the bedroom door. Harry stayed as he'd been, mid-movement, leaning on his elbow. The sound of movement as if by touch rather than sight. A second or two of silence then a practised whine in the front door, which wheezed as a rule. There was a clean wooden crunch as it shut, firmly enough that the catch wouldn't snag in the metal enclosure and require two separate pulls though not so loud that . . . but he was awake anyway.

When they got up in the morning, Bill was where he was when Harry had left him, lying in the living room on the cushions they'd taken off the sofa and lined up on the floor. Pat and Debby walked past him quietly, not daring to look. They ate their breakfast off the kitchen counter and spoke in stage whispers, revelling in the silence. Harry went by quietly too but he glanced over at his brother, the inert mass on the floor, longer than he imagined. As he did so he caught Bill's eyes, following him in the tall window.

§

Bill was out again when Harry came back from college that evening and Pat had left a note to say she'd taken Debby to the park – it was bonanza time for her, at least. He put down his bag and stood in the hallway. The fridge motor started to purr and it was nice to hear it, he thought. Listening as if to a domestic cantata, he took off his jacket, folded it carefully and placed it on top of his bag. He walked into the living room, opening two buttons on his shirt as he went, and poured himself a glass of whiskey from the cabinet. Not older brother behaviour this time, he thought, not particularly good father behaviour either, but good behaviour nonetheless. He seemed to glimpse himself in the life, the living room, he'd imagined. Tending to your own needs was difficult, he thought as he sat back in the sofa and pulled open the paper. Recognising them, then acting upon them, was a skill to be learned. He put

the newspaper down and let his arms drop. The way
pleasure registered itself in your life – it needed permanence, surely, only that could save it from ugly necessity.
Or else you did things that made you forget all about
their continuation or the accursed next time. Music,
maybe, or drugs. He picked up his drink from the coffee
table and took two tiny sips, just enough to tingle his lips.
This was good though – five, ten, fifteen minutes, stolen
in broad daylight, a quarter of an hour which might yet
be infinite . . .

The key in the lock, when he heard it, filled him with
embarrassment – that he might have thought of his time
alone as some sort of relief. From what exactly? It was
Debby and Pat coming home. He heard Daddy in his
daughter's chatter and raced to the door to greet them. He
whisked Debby off her feet and give her a twirl. She held
onto him tight and the smallness of her arms around his
neck felt like a world of meaning all on its own. He kissed
the top of her head as he put her down and, with her still
standing between them, leaned forward to kiss his wife's
lips.

§

Bill came back in time for dinner and they ate solemnly
again. Debby and Pat took their lead from Harry, who

retreated progressively as the evening wore on, acquiescing to the silence as if to an advancing enemy. There was a *Wells Fargo* Western on television which they watched through closing eyes, struggling to maintain the enthusiasm necessary even for sitting together in a room. Harry's shrinking feeling seemed to gather up past sadnesses until it was an actual sadness for the past itself, a chemical disappearance. Brushing arms with Bill on the sofa.

It was what he might have wanted, he thought a little later, to spend time with his brother. Like when he'd come down to see them, Pat and Debby and him, in their first proper place, in Baton Rouge. Weekends they spent talking technique and chord progressions, still in their twenties, and golfing together in green companionship. He'd look forward to showing Bill his recent discoveries like he'd just dug up gold in the garden. But Bill was reticent even then. He never talked about people he'd played with, people Harry might otherwise have revered, except to illustrate specific points, and even those seemed to hover about in some netherworld between expression in his mind and eventual articulation. He had a way of keeping it all for himself, even of making it seem like something they'd discussed and agreed upon beforehand; that he wouldn't explain any more than Harry would understand the explanations.

Now he didn't dare ask. Precious little of it was reasonable, Harry thought, the relationships you had with people.

There'd be silence between them somewhere now whenever they spoke. Evenings that passed quick and empty, dinner and TV, duets made up of two times one, trios three.

Harry heard Bill go out that evening and the next, after lights out. The sound of the door closing, the studied pull, knocked him out of forgetting and bolted him upright in bed. He felt angry, like he wanted to get up and stay up until Bill came back, so that he might tell him about the allowances they were making for him, how they wanted him to succeed . . . Even in that state, however, Harry couldn't sustain his vigour and he went back to sleep assuaged, as it were, by regret. It was what happened, he thought, like some part of Bill had been closed off to them for good. It was just something that happened. But it was still a shame; he only had one brother.

§

The early part of the following week went by in quiz shows, Hitchcock half-hours and more Westerns until, on Thursday, the baseball started up again and they saw the Yankees win, lose and win in Chicago and wipe the floor with Baltimore. Then Harry came home from college one evening to find Bill and Debby sitting together in the living room. Bill was cross-legged on the floor, Debby on the sofa kicking out her legs in front of her. They were chatting comfortably – or Debby was anyway. She was telling him all about a girl called Amy. And Bill was smiling, and his smile carried over into his brother's entrance before them. Harry went into the kitchen where Pat smiled at him too, obviously pleased at the turn of events.

There was no sign of Bill in the living room when they woke up next morning. The cushions were there as before but he was gone. Harry thought immediately of him lying somewhere, stricken, across town in Spanish Harlem, high up on Broadway or in the Bronx, Grand Concourse, Bowery, Canal Street. Debby, all beans and brio in the morning normally, was nowhere to be seen either and the door to her bedroom was shut. They went in to check on her and there was Bill lying on the floor, stricken indeed, but by no worse than sleep, apparently. He was being tended to by Debby, who wasn't perturbed in the least by his presence. She was calmly serving him imaginary lemonade and telling him to sleep, sleep, he needed to sleep, full of efficient kindness.

§

Bill seemed to come to a little after that, even if Debby was the sole beneficiary. He let her play next to him, tapping the free place on the sofa, joining in her games occasionally and chatting sometimes too. Debby was unshakeably proud and every regard thereafter which had about it even the vaguest hint of a smile was vindication, proof that her patient was responding well to treatment.

Pat also seemed to believe in Debby's restorative powers, which wasn't surprising in itself, but she invoked them deliberately one evening, interrupting the news to suggest that they go to the beach at the weekend. Debby gave an excited yay and immediately turned to Bill, to ask with her eyes whether he'd come as well.

Come half-past nine on Saturday morning, then, they were already on the subway out to Brighton Beach, sandwiches and drinks in the wedding-gift cooler, towels, bucket and spade.

There was a salutary breeze blowing up through the narrow streets around the elevated station when they arrived. They walked down the steps and spent a moment in hesitation at the nearest street corner. They all seemed to want to go in different directions and bumped into each other, extending hands onto shoulders and waists as the collective decision made itself known. When they walked on at last, they passed women standing in doorways, looking like their grand-mothers and doting on children playing in the street from distances of eight or ten yards. Over there was the sea.

Debby took Bill's hand and pulled him along at an excit-able pace until they'd built up a decent lead. Harry saw them talking to each other, Bill leaning over slightly towards her, Debby walking on tiptoes.

They set up camp as near as they could to the ocean and laid out their towels, three of them adjacent, like Neapolitan ice cream. Debby played at their feet, building sandcastles and knocking them down, burying herself in the sand and writing her name in letters six feet high. She ran down to the sea, screaming, and came back out telling of how she'd seen jellyfish and treasure.

Bill rolled up his sleeves and opened a button on his shirt. He even took off his shoes. He sat with his arms around his knees but extended his right leg every so often to rub his toes in the sand. There was a tuft of black hair on his big toe which pushed through the epidermis like a carrot sprouting. White, ministerial flesh.

They ate their lunch before midday and dozed for a while after that, propping up the walking-stick umbrella they'd brought with them and lying with their heads towards the handle. Their four pairs of legs poked out from the circle like crosshairs. Harry didn't sleep but he did rest his eyes awhile, letting them shut of their own accord, a red weight on his eyelids. He listened to the others' breathing, their three cadences moving in and out of phase, with each other and with the waves too. The movement came to a shimmering crescendo in sixes and sevens and in another measure which he wasn't able to follow. It gathered in his mind, swelling like cymbals, before coming at last to a crashing release.

Debby stirred before the others and Harry heard her get to her feet. He opened his eyes carefully and saw her looking at each of their faces in turn. When their eyes met, he gave her a wink and a conspiratorial shh.

He must actually have dozed off after that because he was aware suddenly of a stirring beside him. When he looked up he saw that Bill was covered in sand up to his knees and that he was now kicking himself free. Debby was standing over him, laughing. Bill turned onto his stomach and pushed himself onto his feet with a burst of fluid energy no less graceful than it was astounding. He started to jig about on the spot. Then he raised his hands and clenched them into loose fists, at which point he stood still and gave Debby a theatrical glare. Harry looked over at Pat as Bill started jigging about again and circling Debby purposefully. Her face filled with wonderment and she raised her own fists, doing her own little dance on one leg. At Bill's invitation, she aimed a punch six inches wide of his protruding chin and he turned away at the imagined impact, bending double and holding his jaw. When he'd recovered and was standing upright again, he took Debby's hand in his and spat into it two small, white pebbles. She whooped with laughter and lunged forward to hug his legs.

When they'd calmed down again, they went for an ice cream and, mid-afternoon, walked down to Coney Island.

Harry found himself alone with Bill for a while and it crossed his mind that it would be the perfect time to engage him, while he seemed clear and present, a breeze playing around them and only the sea making waves. He couldn't get started, though, or didn't really want to, and that was the crux of it, he thought – a battle of individual desires with the greater will. They walked on in silence.

Debby had talked all day about riding the Cyclone. One of her friends – the same Amy, perhaps – had been on it the previous weekend and had spoken of nothing else when they saw each other in the park. Harry suspected she was less keen to ride it for herself but let her keep up the play for as long as she wanted. When they got close enough to the beast for them to hear its screaming, he saw a clouding in her eyes and it was obvious then that she wouldn't go on it for all the ice cream in the Tri-state area. He felt a tremendous respect for *her* will all of a sudden, the thwarting within, and, as Pat chided her for dragging them all down there unnecessarily, offered her his hand's relief. She accepted and he felt her desolation disperse in him. He wished he could transmit to her, through feeling flesh, such things . . . Hands that knew, in fact, all there might be worth knowing.

§

Debby regrouped quickly enough and, at eight o'clock that evening when they got back, was still as excitable as she'd been twelve hours before. They had a takeaway dinner and sat down in front of the television, glad of having done something at least with this particular day to justify its sedentary denouement. Debby calmed down eventually and they got her off to bed and wondered – a day for departures, after all – whether Bill might not at last have something worthwhile to say to them. As soon as they finished dinner though, the familiar silence descended and even the colours in the room seemed to desaturate. The effect, Harry thought, was like the few minutes that immediately preceded a summer storm. The spectrum flattened out into browns and greys, and you felt the air being extracted from ground level and pumped into pummelling clouds directly overhead. It didn't always rain and on those occasions you imagined – the effect was almost more pronounced than being in the eye of it yourself – the fury being unleashed somewhere nearby, over New Jersey for example.

From the bedroom, they heard Debby call for Uncle Bill – who looked over at Harry immediately. Harry gave him a low nod and he got up from the sofa and made his way to the bedroom. Harry followed and stood at the door as Bill went to sit on the edge of the bed. He leaned forward to kiss Debby's forehead. Sleep tight, he said, his voice soft and kindly.

Debby wanted a story, though, and looked like she was prepared to dig in to get it. Again Bill looked at Harry. Harry gave him another low nod.

Bill leaned back a little and looked around him like he was going to make something up based on the pictures on the wall or as if a story might come to him out of the gloss emulsion. He avoided their eyes as he started to tell Debby about Petrushka the wooden puppet, a story he'd heard when he was about her age himself: the nasty Moor, the ballerina and the magician who brought Petrushka to life so that he'd have all the feelings an ordinary boy might have. Bill told her about the dancing and the Shrovetide fair and about Petrushka trying to escape from his cell. Debby sat up in bed, enraptured, and, still in the doorway, Harry watched her features form in desperate pity for the young boy as he fought the Moor. All the things she was . . . When Bill told her about the night of the carnival, it was almost as if Harry could see on her pupils the flickering images behind them and the dashing horror – spiked with glee – when the Moor killed the young boy with his sword. Bill finished his story by improvising as happy an ending as he could – he told her how Petrushka came back to life and flew high above them all and how everybody was jealous of *him* then. Debby had on her face an expression resembling that which they'd seen when they found Bill sleeping in her room. It was as though she'd read all the subtextual symptoms and had already set about treating them. Debby said thank you and Bill seemed taken aback. It's a very good story, she said then. You tell it well, Uncle Bill.

She laid back after that and turned her head towards the wall, as if to indicate that she was ready to sleep, and Bill leaned forward to kiss her cheek this time. When she felt his face near hers, she turned back towards him. Petrushka reminds me of a piano player I saw in a cartoon once, she said. He was a wooden puppet too. He didn't have fingers and he banged the keys with his fists. He still played well though.

As Bill was getting up from the bed, he stole Debby's nose between his thumb and forefinger. You're a clever one, aren't you, he said, smiling more or less. Debby gave her nose a knowing dab.

§

In bed that night, Harry was woken once again by the sound of Bill's considerate pull on the front door. Or he was awake already and waiting for it. His immediate reaction was the same as before – knocking fear, followed by low-sounding annoyance. This time, he got out of bed and walked quietly to the bathroom. The light burned buzzing vignettes onto his vision and he stood still for a moment for his eyes to adjust, arm outstretched behind him. He felt calm come over him immediately, the change effected as if by the light itself. Something about the hour, man's mastery of the dark and his being awake. Something musical as he unbuttoned himself, urinated and pulled down the lid of the toilet, in lieu of flushing.

His mind went back to Bill's concert, already more distant than the few weeks that had gone by since he'd first thought of it as indelibly past. He wondered how he might have reacted to Scott LaFaro had they actually spoken – and thought again of the contrasting styles he'd witnessed on the bandstand. He imagined himself into the dead man and felt an immense, swirling pity, as it occurred to him that Scotty might have knocked himself out finally on the fine mesh aura that had built up, whether unwittingly or with tacit approval, around Bill. At the same time, trying hard to maintain his poise, he thought of the sport they'd played as children and one word that defined all Bill and he had ever done together. Like they were their own collective noun – a competition of brothers.

§

Harry laid on his side when he got back to bed, facing away from Pat. He didn't feel at all like sleeping any more but the absence was acceptable enough and he spent a while in agreeable non-sensation, looking into the dark not seeing anything, not even with his mind.

When he did fall asleep again, he dreamt that he was full of sawdust and flying over Baton Rouge. Below him were different encampments – some eight or ten in all, he thought, though what they were exactly he wasn't able to say. Each had a different bright colour and a clear demarcating form – square, circle, hexagon, crescent. He was shooting out sawdust from his ears like jet fuel and the trails remained in the air, crystallising then falling gently to the ground. He heard their silvery tinkling far below. He awoke from the dream just as his engine started to chug. Immediately he heard the apartment door being strangled open and cricking like a pitcher's neck. It shut as quietly as ever. Harry listened intently, straining his neck to lift his ears clear of the pillow. He thought he could hear padding footsteps, dragging across the linoleum floor, but it was more likely his imagination, still suspended in dream fluid. After another few seconds, he realised that the idea he had of the next room had become quite inhuman, as though he might open the door onto a scene of unspeakable horror – ritual sacrifice or devilish merriment in which Bill would be grotesque, drugged and all too terribly recognisable.

His next dream was a nightmare but he had the impression that he was fully awake all the while, looking into the dark as before, not seeing the dream images as such but feeling them, in his palms and on the soles of his feet. Bill featured in them now and, in the last, which Harry retained well into Sunday, he was pressing down the plunger on a syringe, injecting himself and pushing his thumb through two fingers like he'd stolen Debby's nose.

§

Things moved quickly after that. Harry found that he couldn't overcome a nasty feeling that he was being incited to drop his brother clean. Come the afternoon, he even stopped trying and let the feeling come as it would.

In the evening, Debby pestered Bill to play her her song, the Waltz for me, so-called. Bill's body seemed to sag at the request and he looked at the floor for a few seconds, during which time Pat tried to come to his rescue. Uncle Bill's tired, she said, he'll play it some other time. Debby persisted, however, and, seeing Pat advance as if to take the situation firmly in hand, Bill gave in.

He struggled initially. It was as if he was weighed down by a deep-seated embarrassment, as well as by everything else. Was that colour in his cheeks? Debby went to stand next to him and watched his fingers intently, mystified that they might move so fluidly and without the slightest hesitation. Then something happened, imperceptibly, and he started to flow.

Harry listened dutifully. It was easy to admire Bill's playing – lithe and canny, a ringing gift in the wood. He stood behind him, looking at his brother's back, at his hands caressing the keys, drawing music from the instrument as if by osmosis. He thought of his own pleasure at the piano, those times when he was able to watch his hands move, for the spectacle of it, to feel his unconscious mind. The doing was the thinking then. Certain parts of certain tunes revealed themselves as odours: the mustard hint in his first girlfriend's breath when she drank Martini, Debby freshly showered.

When the theme came around again Bill played it practically unadorned and Debby hummed along too. The effect, out of the blue, was awful. The head, even as Harry stood there listening, was being stuck down with sentimentality, something maudlin and weepy. And worse – a clogging pity, the music itself condemning Debby to eternal childhood. His bounding, boundless Debby. Harry looked to his right, into the long glass of the living-room window, and there was their father again, watching his boys go at it, as though in his name.

The song came to an end and Debby and Pat applauded. Bill nodded and smiled. Harry felt like he could cry.

§

He'd persuaded himself by Monday morning, sleeping on it hard, that, for Debby's sake, they could no longer have Bill in the house. He was too erratic and might only become more so. Harry didn't like the way saying that made him feel, but he didn't have to like it, he thought, only to bear it until he didn't need to any more. But it wouldn't do in any case to have Debby get used to having her uncle around only for him to leave, at some time of *his* choosing, just as abruptly as he'd arrived. And he obviously needed space and couldn't possibly be comfortable on the sofa. There were plenty of reasons, in fact.

When he got up to campus, he called Mary from a phone booth and suggested to her that it would be good for Bill to get away from it all for a while, really get away. Come down to them in Florida, for example. Mary didn't need persuading, as Harry had known she wouldn't. He assured her that he'd make all the arrangements himself and she was even grateful to him when they rang off.

The following morning, they took Bill and his old leather bag out to Newark. After checking him in and while they were standing around waiting as if for permission to leave, Bill thanked them for their company and for their kindness. Pat told him not to be silly, it was what family was for. Harry wasn't convinced it was the response Bill had been looking for but he didn't say anything. He looked up at him from his shoes to give him what he hoped would be an encouraging nod. Debby was at a friend's.

When they got back to the apartment, Harry had a whiskey and a cigarette at the window. He imagined himself briefly the puppeteer of the incessantly unfolding scene: men sitting out and edging into the sun, awnings and stoops, taxis, full of yellow assertion, jockeying for position. A tooting below made him think of Bill pissing away his talent, disposing of it to pass the time of day. He felt a dull murmur in his teeth and lifted his arm to his head, pushing his index finger into the little nook between his jawbone and the lower part of his ear. At the top end of the block, traffic lights turned from red to green. At the bottom end too, a split second later. He stayed at the window until they'd changed back.

ALL-NIGHT VIGIL
[MARY]

VESPERS

It was already another hot day when Mary awoke. The moist undersheet she'd hung from the curtain rail before going to bed had long since given up its damp cooling and the sun was now going greedily at the fibres, trying to proceed by singeing, to press home its translucent advantage. She'd tried to stay in bed in order to take another half-hour's energy, or as much as she could muster, into the day with her. But her eyes had accepted the light before they were fully open, her ears the smoky *matinale* on Route 1, and there was nothing more to be done.

It was only right, she thought, on her way downstairs, that such a day start early. She might no more have stayed in bed than had it been Christmas and she once again a child of five. Rather than an old woman of three score and. She put the kettle on to boil, took a banana from the fruit bowl and stood by the sink to eat it. She opened the window and wondered, as she wondered most mornings but with particular emphasis today, if she'd be able to hear the ocean.

As the kettle started whistling, she took the scissors from the drawer and snipped open a tea bag. She poured the liberated leaves into the pot and the hot water over them, an act of defiance that had started out small and become a ritual as insurmountable as the samovar might ever have been. She waited a few minutes for her tea to brew, during which time she tried not to let the day's thoughts run away with her. Not yet. Then she poured herself a cup and took it with her through the living room and out to the garden.

She sat on her little bench to watch the light, quite glad now that she hadn't stayed in bed. She let the colours work out their formations before her and tried to imagine what effect, if any, her presence in the scene might be having on its composition. None, in all probability, beyond the fact of her being able to witness it. But what a gift that was to have bestowed on unsuspecting eyes. She tried to keep up with the progression of skipping constants – a canvas that remade itself in perfection every time she blinked, or in instants too fine in reality for her to make the abstraction. When she tried to bear in mind a red that needed all the names of the spectrum just to get close to the way it looked, and still more to describe the way it felt, she realised that she was neglecting orange blues and purple greens of such fervent numinosity that they'd already become a tugging in her. She brought the tea up to her lips and blew across the surface of the liquid, eyes still fixed front.

Their neighbour's black cat walked across the garden, wholly grey against the rapturous green lawn but outlined by a snug-fitting neon halo. It made him look somehow messagerial and she followed his procession into next door's patch where he hopped onto a dustbin then up onto the flat roof of the garden shed to curl up – or stretch out, more probably – in the gathering heat.

Mary looked down into her tea. There were two leaves floating on the surface. One was long and curved, as if it had a joint in the middle. The other was smaller, more round and substantial, and she thought of her two sons, the longer of whom would be home before the end of the day, this last day of July.

§

She went back into the house, to the kitchen sink, where she ran the cold-water tap and rinsed the dregs from the bottom of her cup into the flow. Sunlight was pouring in through the window and the rays caught the brown liquid, turning it into a golden stream which remained quite distinct from the water. When she turned off the tap, there were a few stray drops around the bowl – coming up amber now – and she tried to imagine the time needed for them to stain the white enamel; their quiet, patient work over many years, persisting even when it seemed like they'd all been washed away.

She switched on the radio, just loud enough for her to hear it when she kept still, then went to the little pantry by the front door to get bacon and bread for Harry's breakfast. She caught the headlines and weather forecast at seven o'clock, which promised hot, torrid days to come and included warnings for the elderly and infirm. She put the bacon on to fry and it fizzed violently, too full of water to be any good beyond its taste of pork. The noise bothered her, occupying a range in her mind about an inch above her ears. When it was done she lit the oven to keep it warm for when Harry eventually got up. There was music on the radio now and she hummed along, even though she didn't know the song and had started at least a couple of tones out of tune. She turned it up a notch just as the record was coming to an end and the presenter announced the artist and title. It wasn't anybody she'd heard of and Mary wondered if he'd ever rolled Bill's name over in his accomplished patter.

She washed the frying pan and put away the last of the dishes from the previous evening then went into the hallway with the washing basket to gather up clothes that she'd left on the clothes horse to dry overnight. Harry's shirts mostly, all showing equal signs of wear around the armpits and the fourth button. She folded them in half, mechanically, to make ironing them less tedious later on.

Back in the kitchen, she turned the radio up another notch and let the peculiarly florid breakfast chatter distract her by turns. She heard Harry stirring upstairs now, the creaking in the floorboards a quite integral part of his expression. He'd made them speak his body's language here just as he had in Plainfield. The way some people insisted on acting out their lives, audibly, visibly, for others to know them.

He came into the kitchen and pulled his chair out sharply from under the table, giving Mary a good morning grunt as he sat down. She presented him with his bacon from the oven, butter already on the table alongside toast that seemed to grill to the precise rhythm of his surfacing. Harry went immediately to turn up the radio and the voices moved into the space above the table. Mary sat down opposite her husband, doing nothing as he ate.

She felt relieved in the first place by the radio's persistence. It took up conversations she might otherwise have had to engage in herself. The presenter and his assembled guests were bubbling over with forced gaiety, an energy most unmorning-like in the sense that they wanted it to feel like primetime. In the end, though, with Harry nodding and tutting in agreement or indignation at the least banal proposition, it only served to remind her how much she would have preferred not to have been part of either. She thought of the compromise of married life, a constitution not between their two selves but between hers alone and a capacity to clear things away.

Harry finished his breakfast, pushed his chair back deliberately and gripped the table as he got up to go to the bathroom. Mary knew she could count on him being in there a good fifteen minutes and, before washing up his plate and cup, shut off the radio with a vengeful flick of her thumb.

§

All quiet again, she tried to recall the dawn colours. She poured the rest of the tea from the pot into the sink and it came out the colour of aged bronze this time, a filmy coagulate lining its flow.

She wanted to keep it all to herself for the time being, in the confines of what she knew – morning, dawning anticipation. An excitement that *couldn't* be shared, for fear of its going out like a trick of the light. Keeping it in because the words for it were unknown; breathy substance intervening only to snuff out what was living in it, the sparking of self and soul. She thought of the sea and her mind sped her down empty streets, through red lights and stop signs, placing her in the wash up to her ankles. Twelve feet high with nothing but a moving blue in her eyes.

§

Harry emerged from his ablutions and his presence, under her feet in the kitchen, his breathing as he read the paper, was very quickly intolerable. She sent him into the garden and he accepted the banishment with good grace, perhaps understanding something of his wife's agitation or else acquiescing now so that he might call in the favour later. Mary let her fingers trace the outline of a veneered knot, sitting down again briefly at the table, as Harry went to get his shoes from the hallway.

She caught herself feeling vaguely guilty that her husband should, through no other fault than his own, be allowed such a peripheral part in the day's unfolding. A quick notion that they should be talking, granting to that which they'd built together time's saving grace. Especially now that their scissored history, patched up as it went along, was accruing finally the simple benefit of its having been made. At the same time, in her mind, and in her body too, she recalled the bristling of nights spent alone, when he'd stayed out all night, God knew where, the boys still young. But it wasn't even a question of reproach because, beyond the affront to an assumed wifehood, she'd been glad of that too. The anger had made her feel alive.

Suddenly, entirely, she was back at the orphanage in Old Forge, sitting alongside Justine. The humming of the fridge seemed to bring with it the deep, coated voice of their schoolmaster priest. A resonant, sustaining undertone that held her in its cadence. She felt a deep exhalation of breath in her stomach and the sound entwined with tremors in her mind too, memorial like the strings on a double bass, pulled back hard then held then released, vibrating long and low.

The priest transported them when he sang – into their responses to the liturgy, which they waited for like the good choristers they wanted to be, and the magnificent allure of a life in ritual. Music, such gloried, holy music. Voices shimmering microtonal against the walls, love sight unseen and the Everlasting Father.

§

Morning ticked by, announcing its tasks at convenient intervals. Mary carried them out readily, crossing them off the rolling, self-renewing list. The novelty was only ever in the order of their accomplishment. Come eleven o'clock, it was time to start thinking about lunch and she caught a brief, relieving breeze – time passed differently when there was a pot boiling on the stove.

When at last she called Harry in, she was able to intuit his presence behind her as if by a displacement of the air or the blurred points he occupied in space; his back and shoulders yielding a little bit more each day. They'd be definably old before they knew it, she thought. That is, they'd notice it in the other first and be filled with gladness that they themselves were still more or less intact.

They ate lunch in silence and the sun burned out more and more of the porcelain as they cleared their plates. Harry leaned back in his chair when he'd finished and brought his fist up to his mouth to suppress a burp. Mary looked up. Nothing stuck to him, she thought. He simply went on. He had an ordinary serenity which seemed to come to the surface syphoned from an untroubled core. She, on the other hand, felt precarious, as though her very being ran on alternating motors. There was a perceptible weakening in her arms as she took in their plates and carried them over to the sink.

The tap spluttered when she turned it on and shot out a compacted jet of air before the water came rushing through. The noise made Mary jump and she placed her hands on the edge of the sink to steady herself. She could feel her heart racing. When she'd regained her composure, she felt the need to say something and suggested to Harry that he head out to the airport before too long, even though Bill's flight wasn't due until late afternoon.

§

She tried to keep busy after Harry left. She went upstairs to the spare room and stripped the bed even though the sheets hadn't been used since she'd changed them the last time. After replacing the undersheet, she went around each corner in turn to smooth out the creases carefully. She brought a glass and a little decanter up from the cabinet in the living room and placed them on the bedside table. She thought of putting some of Bill's records on the empty shelves before deciding against it finally, contenting herself with bringing up the copy of *Time* that had been hanging around the house for the past few weeks. There was a paragraph about Stravinsky inside and she hadn't wanted to throw it away. As she left the spare room, she felt a twitch in her left eyelid, two or three determined pulses in the space of a second, and she closed her eyes briefly to let it pass.

Back downstairs, she felt unable at last to rein in her mind. It *did* feel like Christmas – and the fact of picking up an earlier thread gave her an impression of being guided or written out, in an attentive hand. She thought of the Christmases of her girlhood, when she still allowed herself to imagine her father coming home from work, as he must have done when she was too young for the memory to stick. He'd be full of the quickly spent energy of downtime, which they'd latch onto immediately, her siblings and her. A day, day and a half, two if he was lucky. He never came though and it wasn't long after that before she and Justine were at the school for orphans. They spent four years there, as if in an orbit of their own lives, docking only occasionally with the mothership. Mary wondered what her father would have been like, what she would have been like herself had he lived long enough for her to remember some of his being. Bill might not have been at all, of course, and a fear of that order ran in her now, as though she'd sent Harry to the airport to wait for a flight that wouldn't come.

She allowed herself to imagine Bill looking like her father, as if to know them both better. Tall and thin, cheeks chiselled out of a baby face by hard work. What would remain of them, she thought, was bound to be unsaid. It was a much surer thing than anything they'd done or even the things they might yet do. Even beyond the abstract realm. How could her father have existed except in all that he hadn't said to her during fifty-odd years of absence? Like the newspaper clippings Harry sent down from New York and which he addressed to her only. They bore witness to it too, pragmatically, in black on white; forms that were the very negation of Bill's presence and printed for truth on cheap paper. What terrible presumption, she thought. None of those people were there. None of them knew. Let *me* tell you how it was, and she let the words become whispers. She was taken back as she did so, having walked in the meantime into the living room to sit on the very edge of

the sofa, to Bill as a baby and the first time she saw her
eyes in his, when they placed him in her arms wrapped in
a rough towel.

§

She looked out of the kitchen window deliberately and
often as the expected hour came around. When Bill arrived,
though, he caught her unawares. She looked up instinctively – an unwitting few seconds' pause from what she
was doing – and there he was. Standing at the bottom of
their little driveway, dressed dark and holding a brown
leather bag. He was looking down at the ground, like he'd
fallen out of the blue sky and landed on his feet. Then
Harry came into view behind him and he turned towards
the house. He saw Mary in the window and raised his
right hand.

He passed out of sight until the door opened and she
heard them both taking off their shoes in the hallway.
Mary felt herself taken aback by her boy's appearance –
both the way he'd appeared before her and the way he
looked. She told herself that it was only natural; people
never arrived the way you expected them to. They were
always paler or shorter or thinner than you remembered
and you waited then for your mind to catch up. But there
was more to it than that. He did look thin – probably ten

pounds underweight – but he looked like himself too, immediately. That is, he looked like he did as a boy, of whatever age. Like the idea of him she'd always had and which had existed independently, she realised, of all other ideas formed when he wasn't in sight. He also looked, quite unmistakeably, like his living elsewhere, like the fact of his life elsewhere, and Mary felt something at once leaving her and coming back. All the things he did, ways of doing them, about which she knew nothing. Raising his hand or holding a bag, the ways she'd given him to the world.

§

She let him come into the kitchen properly before going to him. His shirt was creased and his embrace held a tired odour – old smoke and sleep not wholly restorative. As they broke, she put her hands either side of his head and pulled him down to her to kiss his cheek. Bill's face flushed as he straightened himself again and Mary looked at him for a long few seconds, as if to inspect his skin or check for other signs, known only to her perhaps, of his well-being. Then Harry came into the kitchen and she motioned to them both to sit at the table.

They were carried initially by the sound of dinner being served – serving spoons and screeching forks. Harry said A little bit more to potatoes and sauce then went about his plate with gusto. For a whole minute his chewing and the way he cut his food with his fork, spooning it up in the same movement, marked out a percussive order. Bill ate slowly, as if to reason with every mouthful, and Mary wondered if and what else he'd eaten that day. Then she looked at Harry and saw that he'd slowed his rhythm to glance up at Bill every so often. She was perfectly happy not talking, she thought, even with Bill at the table, as it became apparent that Harry wouldn't be holding his peace much longer.

How's the Big Apple then, he asked, directing the question at Mary. Bill put his fork down but kept his eyes firmly on his plate. It's OK, I guess. Just OK? Well, it's tough too, but it's OK. You know. If I knew I wouldn't have to ask, would I, Harry said, trying to catch Bill's eye. Couldn't get a word out of him in the car. Still Bill looked down, though, and Harry shook his head. He smiled to himself as he went back to his food and Mary tried to catch her husband's eye now, to convey to him what she could with her eyebrows.

After a while, chewing it over with the aid of a few deliberate mouthfuls – they had the same way of eating, she thought, Bill and her – she broke the silence herself. We were very sorry to hear about your friend. She didn't dare look up. But we don't have to talk about it, not unless you want to. Relax. Let us look after you a bit. She tried to give this last phrase a more jovial inflection and Bill responded with a half-hearted smile. Mary felt pity for him and for herself too, coming together in a sense of the mystery she'd engendered in his being.

§

After dinner they went into the living room and Mary felt herself relaxing a little. It felt at least a little like Jersey and, as such, like home. She brought in tea on a tray.

Harry sat back in his chair and tugged some of his shirt out from the waist. He opened another button at the neck and the television news announced that it had been a record day in Florida – a round one hundred. Harry gave a dramatic Phew. Thirsty work, eh? He went to the cabinet in the corner of the room and took out two glasses and a bottle of whiskey. Your mother won't mind. We've both mellowed in the Florida sun, haven't we, Mare? Sweet as oranges now we are. And it's a special occasion anyway, isn't it. He gave Mary a wink and poured two indulgent measures.

The evening went by quietly. Harry attempted conversation and soldiered on gamely for a while, remaining quite amiable even when he found responses unforthcoming. He refilled his own glass a couple of times and topped up Bill's too, even though the first had stayed where it was, untouched. Mary saw the same television commercials pass before her eyes four, five times or more, chiming like refrains. She found herself wanting to respond to them, as though to antiphons, with whispered joy. They had a logic in any case – something soulful – quite apart from the products being hawked.

Eventually, Harry started to doze. The glass in his hand hung dangerously over the arm of the sofa and Mary went over to take it off him. When he opened his eyes and saw her standing there he looked docile and grateful. He pulled himself onto his feet then and said goodnight. Best be off to bed, eh? Good to see you, Billy.

§

Bill and Mary stayed as they were. They heard Harry on the stairs then walking across the landing. Water running through pipes then the flushing toilet. The sound moved through the air above them like a swooping fly.

Mary thought of Bill and of her mother now. She tried to recall the relationship they'd had before the boys were born but it was harder to make the leap than she might have imagined. Her mother too had mellowed as Harry and Bill grew up – perhaps because she'd witnessed their growing at first hand and discharged as she did so the burden of her own parenting. All the previous obstinacy, the guilty – or perhaps necessary – pride seemed to let go of her as she saw Harry first then Billy come through safe and well before her. It was all she'd wanted for her own children, wasn't it? Wasn't that the greatest gift she might have given them? Even before Ivan, even before their poor youngest, who never even had a chance. So that if she insisted on speaking to her grandchildren in Russian it was only because she loved them first and foremost in a communion with the motherland. Mary and her siblings had grown beyond that, because there wasn't any other way – but that was also their mother's encouragement, as if it was a will within her and she powerless to overcome it. As Mary herself had been powerless, when the time came; allowing Billy, pushing him too when he needed pushing, to be that which his parents might least understand. A direct derivative of efforts and sacrifices. You made them *for your children*. But when they actually bore fruit it was something astounding: beliefs you would have said were yours all along, so alive had they become in your own flesh and blood.

Are you OK, Billy? Mary felt the words come out freely at last. I'm OK, Bill said, though he looked in fact quite defenceless. It's a hard time. I know, Mary said, I know.

She went to sit next to him on the sofa and reached her arm around his shoulders. Bill leant into her, not so tall now, and she was able to bring her other arm about him too.

§

They went upstairs. On the way, Mary called by the hallway to get Bill's bag but Harry had already taken it up. She felt another brief pang for her husband.

On the landing, she took a sheet from the airing cupboard then went into the bathroom, where she soaked it in the basin and wrung it out, piece by piece, as best she could. She heard it dripping on the carpet behind her as she carried it over to the spare room.

Bill was sitting on the bed when Mary went in. Not like Plainfield, is it, she said, and again she tried to inflect her words jovially. Bill's smile was fuller this time. I haven't been sleeping all that well anyway these last few weeks. Mary stood still for a second, then went back to the bathroom, to the cabinet, where she emptied two white pills from a brown glass bottle into the palm of her hand. Back in the bedroom, she handed them to Bill then went to the bedside table to pour him a glass of water from the decanter. Swallow these, she said. They're your father's. She must have said it in a particular way, though, because Bill looked specifically for her eyes to thank her. Mary kissed him on his forehead.

When she'd turned out the light on the landing and was pushing down the handle to go into her own bedroom, she realised she was beaming.

MATINS

Head on the pillow, Mary said a prayer for her son, combining a verse of her own making with certain from the Psalms, which she tried to match as closely as possible in style and syntax. She took particular care to enunciate the words in her mind, as though they were more likely to get through well thought than well spoken. When she got to the end, Lord have mercy, she doubled up, mouthing the words quietly and deliberately, trying at the same time to clear her mind of everything else. Harry's breathing was long and deep and his inhalations came to a wheezy note. She slept awhile.

When she awoke, an hour or two later, she had a line of the Third Psalm in her mind. I awake, for the Lord sustains me. She pushed a foot free of the sheets and let it hang over the edge of the bed. Harry's breathing was glutinous now but bearable, as if he was snoring at the far end of a larger room.

Mary wondered if Bill was asleep and her mind took

off, to look down on them going about it, on beds of straw, like animals in their boxes. Poor thing, she thought, and she imagined him tossing and turning, tormented and tired and taut. She replayed his arrival – the in-between hour and nature of his appearance that afternoon. It struck her that she'd left something quite fundamental out of her earlier reckoning and that that something was the night itself, or brought to bear, in any case, by night. Something that was the antithesis of daylight – even the exalted light of dawn. That something wasn't darkness, however, more the negation of sight. You couldn't see your body, that was part of it, as was the fact of seeing distance all but obliterated. It was as if you could feel your way, suddenly, around a house whose walls were only as they were because you thought them so.

But only traces of the structure remained come the morning. Impulses that were archaeological suddenly, like ancient footings, and visible only from above, in the weeds that had abounded in the meantime. They existed not to inform daylight and activity but to sit in permanence outside of them, a faint calling across distances that had reverted by then to their habitual calculations of non-arrival.

Mary turned onto her side, towards Harry, and tucked her elbow in tight to her belly even though the bed was big enough and her husband surprisingly respectful of the division of space. It was an instinct of long ago, she thought, as she let her arm relax and her palm press against the sheet. Harry and Bill between them in bed, as likely as not to suffocate under folds of errant flesh. That was the fear, in any case, when it occurred to you suddenly that you had to unlearn your entire body for it to take on new cares.

Bill was a few months old when he rolled out of bed, one night up in New Jersey, and Mary felt the panic coursing through her now as it had then. He didn't fall particularly far but her instinct told her that they'd broken him, never to be put back together. She stayed up all night, breathless and perched on the edge of the bed. She listened as his sobbing subsided in time with her own, giving way eventually to exhausted sighs. After that her mind went black.

Come the morning, they were at the surgery at least half an hour before it opened. The doctor told them that Bill was just fine, that he'd suffered no lasting damage, and they were back at home in time for what was, even with the excursion, an early breakfast. Mary's panic didn't budge, though, and in the weeks that followed, she'd wake up in the middle of the night, or find herself rushing up to his cot as she hung out the washing, to check that he was still asleep and in one piece. She even woke him sometimes, so that he cried, and his sobs reminded her in even more vivid terms then of her negligence.

The feeling seemed to last, in some form or another, throughout his childhood. Different with Bill, despite his being the second son. Harry was mechanical. He needed her energy. Her love too but her physical attention, first and foremost. By the time they had Bill, though, she already had two years' head start and it had dawned on her – the turn of phrase was quite apt – that they might form their boys too, *influence* them. The fear, then, was a fear not for an arm or leg but for Bill's head – and all the more injurious for being the first of who knew how many to come.

She bathed him the day after the accident and spent longer than usual running her fingers through his hair, working them with delicate insistence over his doughy crown. She felt the act itself grounding her, grounding her flesh, in a contact of life and love. She called him Vasyl, as her mother had since his birth, and allowed herself to imagine him that which had seemed unattainably distant the night before: a man full-grown.

The feeling seemed to last throughout Bill's childhood because when he broke his wrist, some years later, Mary nursed him in his room, with music, for him to do more than merely recuperate this time. When she laid with him on the bed, not knowing whether she was curling into him or he into her, she imagined writing him letters in which she'd try and coax him into accepting the world – not for what it was but for what it could be with him in it. You have only to want it, my beautiful dear boy, to put your mind to it, for it to be yours. She imagined getting postcards in return, a few weeks later, from wherever he might be by then, in which he'd tell her that he was getting on well, that he had friends and ideas and energy. The cards would dry up eventually – or so she'd hoped, for she'd know then that he was making his way.

Mary pushed back the sheet just enough to be able to slide her legs out of bed, plant her feet on the carpet and sit up. She replaced the sheet behind her carefully – but Harry slept much better these days, even when he hadn't drunk before bed. She felt for her slippers with her feet and, having found them and put them on, walked over to her mother's chair where her nightgown was hanging over the back. She walked to the bedroom door, trying not to imagine impediments to each step or that Bill was actually in an awful mess.

Out on the landing, she stood still and listened out for sleep breathing. The door to the spare room no longer shut properly, even though the house had been newly built, Harry and her the only occupiers, and the room itself largely unused during the few years they'd been in Florida. She edged towards it and stood still, straining forward to get her ears as near as possible to the opening. Not a sound. All the same, she imagined looking through the door and catching Bill's eyes, a pale white in the darkness, staring right at her. Even the presentiment, the thought that he might be capable of frightening her . . .

Just at that moment, she heard a sound like a butterfly's wings beating against a windowpane. Bill's breathing was short and rapid – but he was sleeping. She recognised the rhythms as those of his early years, when the nightmares ran in reels behind his eyes and she looked down on him, wishing she could take the terrors on herself. She placed the tips of her fingers in the middle of the wood and pushed, just hard enough to start the motion. The agitation in the room covered the door's creaking but Mary remained on her guard, peering around the doorframe that the opening might pass for incidental should Bill hear it and come to.

Walking into the room, it felt briefly as though she were violating something hard-coded. She went in anyway, staying door-side initially. She couldn't make out Bill's form – he was quite calm again now – but looked into the darkness, intuiting his bulk in the sheets. She took three steps to her left to stand at the foot of the bed.

The silence settled around her and she waited for Bill's subconscious to get used to her presence. When she was satisfied that he wouldn't wake up merely as a result of her being there, she went further into the room to sit in the wicker chair between the bed and the window. She lowered herself into it gently and the twigs groaned, as though having the breath squeezed out of them. She clenched her buttocks, halting her movement for a split second.

As the last of her weight transferred onto the seat, the bed started to tremble. Bill's breathing became rapid again, the butterfly butter*flies*, their escaping instincts multiplied tenfold. Mary bolted upright in the chair, petrified. Another frozen second and she heard the vibration in Bill's arms and legs too, as well as in the springs and mattress.

After the initial shock, she leaned back slightly, control-ling the movement from the base of her spine, and listened. She felt immediately that it was precisely this that had occasioned her sleeplessness.

Some minutes went by in which Mary felt her worry profoundly. She thought again of the postcards she'd im-agined writing. They seemed to betray her now – as though she'd set about romancing quite deliberately the mother–son bond. She shook her head. The very idea of sending him out into such a world . . .

And she wondered what it was she wanted of Bill's coming to stay with them. Something perfectly simple at base, she thought. No more than his being with hers, as it had been. To see him in the sitting room, next to his photo on the wall, and in the kitchen. To hear him breathe or see the drift of his eyes into hers.

She thought of her mother again, her father too, and their separate odysseys to the New World. Two boatfuls of nasty smells and hope, spilling out of every orifice. Their meeting in a backwater then to raise a family in poverty and death, speaking no English but still feeling that they were better off there than anywhere else. The whole thing would have been wholly unconscionable, Mary thought, had it not been, in the fullness of something mysteriously American, for Bill.

Whose breathing had eased in the meantime only to quicken again now, bringing Mary back into the room with a start. She pulled up her chair to be closer to him and wondered if she might take his hand or stroke his arm. Something seemed to be urging her forward, a trembling that insisted on being hers as well. What was it, in a touch that he wouldn't even register? Something animal, she thought, not sentimental, which made her think at the same time of an evolution inside her – whole swathes of consciousness that had been unavailable to her but which she'd come upon again, like late-flowering love, in Billy. In the influence she might have had on him and the regard, for himself and for his gift, that she'd hoped to instil. All things she'd learned for herself only when it became a question of their transmission. The formulation struck her as a true meaning of inheritance – deep, humane giving, of things which you got back with blessings – and she imagined circles of reciprocal, responsible joy spreading out and into her, from and into the world.

The vision took her back, once again, to the Old Forge of her childhood – where it clouded over immediately. Her mind repopulated with hardened beings, going about difficult, tainted lives. Animal too, of course, and every bit as inevitable. Christmases brought the tableau into relief and she thought of those she'd spent with her brothers and sisters. They sang together and ate walnuts, which crumbled under blows from the little hammer whether rotten on the inside or not. And from there it was only a measured world of difference to the celebrations Harry and she had prepared for their own children. Harry always went overboard. He wanted them to have everything, there and then, whereas Mary would have preferred to see the boys come into it gradually, the condition of their release. The whole season, leading up to the day itself, seemed to come draped in low-lying fog, a pity which she tried to wear as lightly as possible – so that it didn't have a chance to settle, this notion that they'd only be allowed up for air, and to assert their humanity finally, by way of the gifts they bought. Not that she didn't like being able to give the boys what they wanted either. Comics or model cars, a train set one year; the way they hugged her afterwards . . . But there precisely was the danger. Nothing was sadder than seeing children forced to bear the burdens of deprivation or restricted ambition. There'd be time enough for that later on, it didn't need their best years too . . . But the burden was passed on and accepted anyway, and not always unwillingly or unwittingly. And that was easily the worst of it: nothing more objectionable, or plain sad, than those who before they'd made it even a tenth of the way in had already taken for their own the dirty work.

The Evans celebrated at the same time as other American families – Harry wouldn't have countenanced anything else – but Mary insisted on making them a special dinner on the 6th too, as well as another, in between, for St Basil's. Billy's name day, as it might have been.

He asked for a copy of *Petrushka* one year and Mary was more than happy to oblige. It would be a material contribution to his goodness. Bill was delighted when he unwrapped the disc on Christmas morning and listened to nothing else for weeks on end. They listened together too and Mary was able to see in her son something more consequential than mere pleasure or curiosity. He listened over and over to certain passages, picking up the needle and replacing it with the precision of a dedicated being.

After that, she kept a lookout for little signs, which she counted as personal triumphs. The way he hummed harmonies, trying to make single notes follow each other in such a way that they'd resemble chords, to his ear at least. Even the way he brushed his teeth, contemplating his smile and the bony outcroppings in his gums, as though to try and see his face from the outside.

And all the while, his talent was evolving, his facility for music welling up, in his discretion and in his reserve. The way it made him happy but the way it made him sad too. The music nourished him deeply, refreshing the parts other tears couldn't reach.

The room fell silent as Bill's trembling subsided again and Mary listened gratefully to the absence. As it deepened, she remembered the silence that followed the doxology, after the chorus's last notes. The harmonies remained in the air in such purity that it made you think of their proper expression being precisely that voicelessness. They started to decay eventually but even then the effect wasn't lost. The sublime seeped into the walls and from the walls back into the room. Until those waves decayed too, to reveal at last the one true location – the singing of your own soul, which wouldn't decay, not the least hanging note, until all was released, all carried over.

She'd wanted to take Bill out of the world, she thought. That was her goal all along. Out of localised hardships – Pennsylvania, New Jersey – and out of the greater patchwork too. Gifts and ingratitude, immodesty, all the capital crimes. To allow him access at least to a different world. One in which he wouldn't be obliged to remake the imperfect cycle. She thought of Justine and herself at school, leaning into each other after their father's death and talking it all out, to reproduce as they did so the whole sad story. Copying out the generations. Again Mary tried to see Bill through the dark and she reached out her hand now as though decided at last that she'd touch him. She drew a long, sustaining breath and held it. Bill had music.

Just as her fingers seemed to come into his glow, the bed started to shake again, with a force made all the more violent this time by her proximity. She felt Bill's muscles clenching hard and his whole body seemed on the verge of breaking into spasms. His teeth grinding against each other sounded like chipped millstones. Mary stayed as she was, leaning forward, her hand suspended just above the right angle. She thought of Petrushka, more alive at the end of his story than any of the other characters, and cursed, of course, but touched too from on high.

Billy had come home to them, a man full-grown, to tremble in his sleep. Like Harry used to. But Bill wasn't Harry – he was stronger, better, wiser. He took his wages in other notes. Mary felt her responsibility deeply, her son's being seemingly indissociable in even the tiniest detail from her own. And the dominant note all of a sudden was pride, which came upon her long and surging. I did that, she thought. All that was me.

Eventually, Bill's body became calm again and he turned onto his side, face towards his mother in the dark. The movement seemed somehow definitive. His left arm fell onto the mattress with a springy thud and Mary leaned back in her chair. She closed her eyes and it wasn't long after that before she too was asleep.

THE FIRST HOUR

There was a stirring beside her when she awoke which she
took initially for one of Harry's sleep rituals. The one in
which he turned from his side onto his back, quite deliberately, then back onto the side he'd only just rejected. It
was usually accompanied by a series of out-breaths delivered
as though they were to be his last. They weren't forthcoming
this time, though, and their absence, along with a sudden
awareness of her back slanting onto something hard, gave
Mary to realise that she'd fallen asleep in Bill's room.

She opened her eyes, expecting it to be fully light, and
was amazed to find the room brighter than night by only
grey degrees. Immediately she recalled the impression of
having come up against something deep-seated and inviol-
able as she first entered the room. She got up from the
chair in one movement, surprised herself with her agility
and made as though to walk out. At the foot of the bed
she stopped, as she had earlier, and once again waited for

the silence to settle around her, for her presence to seep unseen into Bill's.

His breathing seemed hyper-regular now by comparison, as though his body had never known anything else. Mary listened to the rise and fall in his chest – like rolling hills seen from afar, broccoli trees in line abreast along the brow. When their two rhythms came into sync, she found herself unable not to concentrate on her own breathing. The way it sped up or became louder simply as a result of her noticing it. She had a sudden glimpse, in conflation, of the day just gone: dawn light and nagging love, fears stratified by housework then later by dark and excavated piecemeal in the spare room. She shivered at the thought of Bill in New York, working late and emerging into doctored night to sleep until the afternoon; that he'd only ever see dawn from the wrong side.

Mary looked to her left. There was a diffuse glow in the sheet hanging at the window, a faint aureole not surrounding anything yet and which was visible when she let her eyes cross but disappeared into the fabric as soon as she tried to bring her attention to bear on it. She thought of the world behind the window, a ragged assemblage brought to life, albeit with infinite patience, as the grey waters receded around. Deserted streets and intersections, their passage through night assured by an oily refraction of red through green, red through green. She shut her eyes, as though to let herself be thought into being anew.

§

When next she opened them, the room was primed for daylight. There was already a long vertical shadow on the wall, separating out the part of the room closest to the window and that in which Bill was still sleeping soundly. She could see oxygen bubbles in the decanter on the bedside table, as if the water itself was beaded with sweat.

Mary tried to recall the thoughts that had occupied her so robustly during the night but felt them flee her, puffed out even as they seemed most likely to re-form. In their place sat a peculiar feeling of having been led into them as though into a trial – of all she hadn't said over the years, and all the small daily hopes that had sustained or deceived her at their pleasure, staining her slowly before being drained off into some dank reserve. She thought of her father and how she cried when they told her of his death. The recollection was colder this time, though, just as she'd felt empty imme-diately afterwards, like she'd never be able to cry again. It already felt like the first step on the way to forgetting, to making her life without him, as if crying itself were the expiation of sin she had no right to be rid of. And she'd kept it all to herself since then, she thought, in order to build herself up. To be strong enough for her life's work – albeit on the silent condition that it all come pouring out again one bright hereafter day.

She got up gingerly from her chair and walked to stand at the window. She peered out through the gap between the sheet and the frame and saw a light come on in an upstairs window across the street. Someone getting up early for work, perhaps, to exert himself in the service of a welcome-home whiskey. Mary had a feeling for the machinery of lives, fed with fuel nobody would be able to extract afterwards; for parents, like her own mother, who went to live with their children, to see their long travails reduced to a share of chicken and potatoes. Or for Harry, asleep in the next room, who'd wanted to be rich, poor devil, but wouldn't have had the first idea how to employ the money he made in his own service. Her own life had been built, in essence, around the home in Plainfield that was just long enough in her making for them to trade it in come the time for nominally beachside modesty. But the back lawn was coming up green now and the houses all the way along the street had been drenched, from one instant to the next, in blameless white.

She turned into the room again and drew back the sheet on the window, for more of the soft, soothing light to penetrate the room. As she walked towards the bed, able at last to make out Bill's features, it no longer felt in the least bit strange that he should be laid up in the spare room of an unfamiliar house. It was the new start that Mary had envisaged and that Bill so obviously needed. She imagined him waking up to find both of them slightly, subtly different.

The sun came directly upon Bill's face at last, falling aslant onto pointed cheeks and his still slicked-down hair. The impression was of his features coming into three dimensions out of two, moving towards her with iconic force. She felt a last reverberation of guilt as she realised that she'd included his trembling, distressed body in her sleepy pride of the night just gone. But even that only served to redouble her determination. For mildness is come upon us, she said to herself, and we shall be chastened.

She whispered a wordless prayer for her boy then walked, full of purpose, out of the room and onto the landing. In the bathroom, she splashed cold water on her face then went downstairs to the kitchen, deciding on the way to make pancakes for breakfast.

THE COLOUR OF SAYING
[HARRY SR]

THE BLUE AND THE GREEN

Hurricane season is a slow yield that summer of 1961 and
they've already had some six weeks of it by the time Bill
comes down to them. Days start out agreeable and enticing
to end up full of damp annoyance. Their clothes, sodden
under the armpits when they take them off at last, are heavy
with the energy they might have deployed during the day in
kindness – but they can do nothing by then except lie there
in the dark, unmoving. And come the new morning, the skies
are as full of promise as ever, tarnished only by odd clouds,
which flutter angelic all the day long as though to conceal
by wispy smokescreen the devilment they might just as readily
put forth. Florida is by turns tetchy and stuporous, gaudy
around certain corners then burnt out, osseous and limed.

Neither is Harry, whose internal barometer hovers as a
rule around fair, insensitive to the spike. For some time,
until he has no other choice but to submit, the heat seems
to transform into an added weight that he can manage,

passing it like an oversized suitcase from hand to hand, but never set down. His movements are laboured, his body beset by skirmishes in what he fears will be a developing battle. He notices his hands particularly, picking up teacups, and the way he falls into chairs, gravity at once pushing and pulling him down, plucking him clean out of the air. Chronically incapable, after that, of keeping his eyes open in front of the television.

Bill's arrival in their midst strikes him as a product of the high pressure, like they've been building up the whole of July to that too. But even then the weather shows no sign of breaking and Harry finds himself beholden, like the beleaguered farmers of his ancestry, to the weather forecast; praying for a drop of rain, as if to supplement his unspectacular pension with the tomato plants he has withering nicely out the back. And the more days that pass like that, unquenched, the more it feels like a rerun of his first summer in retirement. The impression gathers in veracity until it is unmistakeable, infiltrating his internal chemistry too – a feeling that the heat might actually be depriving his organism of vital nutrients, melting his inner workings, and in such a way that they are no longer the same when they harden again after. That was how it felt, in any case, when they moved down the coast. Something uncoupling, or breaking down, as though they were required to skip across the platform and change trains before continuing their onward journey.

He was taken by a name, in the first place, and by the way it sounded out loud. Even the phrase, We'll retire to the sun – not to mention the entailed validation of a career well managed – sustained him during a good part of his working life. More than a simple idea, it seemed to be the corner in which he'd come into his own at last. He spent regular intervals imagining himself speaking modestly in the kind of company he'd never normally keep – precise, well-to-do men and women, to whom he'd deprecate the dirty thrill of business in favour of solid contentment. We couldn't imagine going back now, could we, Mare? As a result, all became subsumed in the one word, Florida – a sunshine state of mind, wherein Ormond Beach or Volusia County, even their street or the house itself, his and Mary's retirements separating out into garden and kitchen, were merely apparatus.

He was less surprised than he cared to admit then when, surrounded at last by reality set in concrete and cracks, it became apparent that he missed New Jersey quite badly. The green of their new lawn wasn't at all like the old one; it was less blue, less grey, just green. The sun obliterated all that was mottled or in any way irregular. He missed work too: the constant flow of people to be silver-tongued and the total absence, from one day to the next, of an audience.

He spent the first few months going out of his way to scuff things up. He wore his shoes in the house and put his feet up on the sofa. He let oil in the garage drip through the car's underbelly onto the concrete floor and deliberately left wardrobe doors ajar in the bedroom for them to warp in the heat. He told himself often and indignantly that he was a Welshman and not cut out for a tropical climate or lounging about in self-satisfaction, countering with the same breath that that was just what they wanted him to think and he'd be damned if he let himself go the way of all the other poor beggars. He felt lonely all the same and abandoned to the mercy of his thoughts, which existed suddenly in lieu of conversation. One thought in particular: that it might have been for this he spent so many years planning, saving, dreaming.

If he finds his feet in the meantime, it is because he can hardly bear not to. He can walk awhile, late afternoon, and have a drink at the bar on the intersection with Route 1, read the paper or pass the time of day with whoever else is there. Try not to think himself up the road, up the seaboard. Or drink too much. Or get in the car, nice and early, golf clubs on the back seat already, and hack his way around a few holes, then a few more, down by the ocean. Not so bad at all. And this, precisely, is what Bill brings with him; Florida can breathe again, as though to exist only when Harry has someone to tell it to.

§

He takes full advantage of the licence to talk. Mornings are an opportunity, to be indulged anew, lunch an unfolding pleasure. Even afternoons, so often spent counting down to his evening drink, can be syncopated now with the offbeat. More, better than anything else, *this* is what he does, he thinks.

He potters about in the garden, Bill sitting out too – on Mary's bench, smoking and looking glum. Harry stops every so often to trap him in the state of things, asking questions not in the expectation of obtaining full or otherwise engaged answers but to include him, simply enough. A notion, which Harry allows to germinate – now that they are both of them too old to teach each other new tricks – of a brotherhood between them. He talks sport and TV, politics and weather, relieved to feel himself approaching the full twelve to the dozen again. It occurs to him once or twice that he should rein it in somewhat, let Bill come to at his leisure, but he can't help himself, nor does he particularly want to.

Kennedy, on the other hand, is more than fair game. He isn't to be trusted. More than any other Collins. Harry's resentment of the Irish is long-standing and doctrinaire, a reproach that hasn't changed in more than four decades. It amounts, in essence, to their failure in 1916 to usher the Uprising over the sea to Wales. It would have been the perfect time, Harry says. The English were occupied elsewhere and wouldn't even have cared that much anyway. And now, the same selfish Micks have taken America, which they'll carve up between them, mark my words. Starting with Boston. As if all they wanted all along was a New England. So don't give me that Celtic cousins bullshit. I was in my prime then. In my twenties. I'd have gone back in a flash.

Or else it is lawnmowers or leaf-blowers. Halogen lamps. Castro – right over there, pointing – or the Russian they sent into space. All the things he's seen, making or breaking America, the greatest country on earth. After the home-land, that is. But that's different. You can't judge them on an equal footing. One is milk and honey, the other life itself.

All the while, Bill says nothing. He sits on his bench, smoking cigarette after cigarette, looking glum.

§

If the last few years have seen talk yield, by and large, to thought, it is with curiosity, then, and a little trepidation, that Harry hears the cadence of mind come through in his speech.

He and Bill spend time together, by default more often than not, having to happen to be in the same space, but it is far from unpleasant. Even his dead-air chatter seems to take on extra significance. Breathing and talking, paying no particular attention to one or the other. But it is at these moments, at his most inane, that Harry feels best able to channel his son, as though the passage of air and sound were acting, in fact, to free up his conscious being.

He tries to see Bill through the prism of other men he's known over the years. The young fellow who worked a few summers at the pool hall in Dunellen, before disappearing between one shift and the next never to be heard of again. They put him down to booze and not eating and Harry remembers the rumours circulating even then of his clinking like a Mexican donkey when he slung his army-issue bag over his shoulder at the end of a shift. At least Harry never had to sack him. Bill has something of that look too, like he might accept an invitation to dinner and take three courses in brandy. But that doesn't seem entirely right either and something classless about booze gives Harry a guilty nudge. It occurs to him that it might well be worse than that, that if it were only booze . . . Whatever it is, though, it is exacerbated by grief and a reticence that seems to have long since taken up residence in his reactive mind – a solid ball, dense and crusted over. And Harry is less surprised by that too than he might have been, back when all he wanted for his boys was for them to learn like him, the hard way, to hustle.

When he breaks again from his gardening and they cling, in close consort, to the shade at the side of the

66666666

house, he wonders if he isn't acquiring finally some small measure of wisdom. Later on, contemplating the grass which he cuts as though shaving the face of the earth, the idea crosses his mind again. When it has formed for the third time in the space of a single afternoon, it is no longer to be doubted and Harry feels like laughing. Like telling someone too. But something in Bill's eyes dissuades him this time and, just as suddenly, it is obvious that if wisdom it be it is precisely Bill's doing. An unexpected gift: how kind of him to bring his father to life again, despite himself.

Harry lets the humility define in him a plan of action. He will talk enough for two and in that way help Bill out. Talk to him in such a way that he understands he isn't required to answer. Form a blanket around him. He knows his boy, Harry thinks, better than anybody, because he knows what it is to want and need. Taught him all he knows . . . And, for as long as Bill is with them, he can use that knowledge to watch out for him, keep him out of harm's way, as if to vouch for him with his own imperfections.

§

They go out golfing together, driving down to the course and skirting the ocean for a mile or so, leaving behind the trailer parks and dollar-dinner motels. The fading billboards at the roadside, bunched together in concerted protest on the outskirts of town, appear less frequently after a while and something lifts in the car too. The galloping sky to their right.

When they turn off the main road, the clubhouse appears briefly through the sabal palms to provide them with a fleeting glimpse into another era. The building itself is modestly ornate – two storeys and a verandah, colonial posts and a pavilion roof – and disappears again almost immediately. Around the next corner it comes into plain view and Harry lifts his eyes from the road for maybe a whole second. The scene inspires in him a particular kind of nostalgia – entirely unrelated to lived experience but full-blooded nonetheless. He imagines himself a wealthy émigré, of the kind Wales never produced, but which might have come into being had the 1916 Revolution gone ahead. Had he been of wealthy parentage and condemned thus to regret for all time the disinheritance.

They park up and Harry goes off to the clubhouse to pay for their game. When he comes back, waving two vouchers in front of his chest discreetly like he's stolen them off the counter, they open the boot and change into studded shoes. Their two sets of clubs lean on the bumper, irons specked here and there with rust. One of the bags is probably Bill's anyway, from all of a childhood ago, dug out that very morning from the depths of the garage.

It is late afternoon, hot and sunny-still, but more

agreeable now. Less prickly. They walk together to the first tee and the crunch of their shoes in the gravel makes them sound content, if not happy.

§

Warming up, Harry suggests they play for a quarter a hole and Bill agrees. Harry invites him to play first and his movements on the tee are somewhat inhibited. His swing, though, still has the trusted purr of a reliable engine and, even without going at it full tilt, he sends the ball down the fairway.

Harry launches himself into his first shot, overbalances, and almost falls over. Undeterred, he tries the same approach again. He makes contact this time and the ball heads off after Bill's only to deviate at the last into a first cut of rough.

He knocks his ball down the fairway after that with largely powerless effort. Bill too seems to be giving it his best and, as they get into the swing of it – set-up, address, action – the game is a problem admitting of no others. No bad thing, Harry thinks, his earlier observation holding firm.

After a few holes, they start to play like they would have played when they were younger, had they not been so overrun by competition and heat of a quite different kind. Swinging for the rhythm of it, up and down, back and through, like aged pendulums. Advancing the ball far enough down the fairway at last for them to haul their bags onto their shoulders and exert themselves walking after it. And that too feels good. Walk pause walk.

There is time between shots now for thought and Harry verbalises at least some of his – on the greens, when Bill and he come together again, or on the walk to the next tee. What comes out of his mouth, however, is still mired in the confrontation of old. You have to get into their heads. Play the man not the ball and, when he wins a hole, he makes sure of informing Bill of the running total. Fifty cents, seventy-five.

For the next few holes, he is preoccupied with whether Bill sees him differently in Florida or whether he is, in fact, just like he used to be in New Jersey. He plays over the years he spent scheming and planning, sometimes prospecting in a specific area though more often than not setting out on the hoof in search of quick dollars. At the pool hall, the driving range, he talked thirteen to the dozen to pull off his schoolyard trades. The man who brought chalk for the cues, for example, driving out from Newark a few times a year, threw in an extra box free if he arrived at lunchtime and Harry served him a beer. Or the fellows, the chaps, the boys, the men, whose composition over the years evolved like George Washington's axe, but who fell in line just the same, into Harry's jokes and greetings, so long as their whiskey sodas were fresh.

How odd does he look down here, he wonders, away from the grit and the grime, all the matted layers of frustration – which suited him so well ultimately, did they not? Enthusing about their escape to the sun while his very being seeps into his shirt. He wishes he were dependable and firm, like his father, and thinks of the skies over New Jersey, when he left work on summer evenings. Looking up on his way home as though to take the backlit blue into his low being.

He makes a nice putt on the fifth green and lifts his eyes to forty-five degrees. There is a plane in the magnified distance, going away from them over the Atlantic. Its engines are pumping out what seems, for as long as he stands there watching, to be the only tangible of time – pink-candied trails fuzzing up in the haze and lasting just long enough to connect recent *a* with nowhere *b*.

§

Around the turn and into the back nine, Harry is up a dollar or so and playing all right. When I was drinking, he says, as though to keep his mind from meddling in his swing, what I wanted more than anything was to have been dry for forty days already, not forty-eight hours. That was the worst – the thought of having to build up to it, work at it every day, which would be too hard. So you didn't start at all. Then a few weeks later, you found yourself thinking, if only you'd started when you meant to, you'd already have done a month by now. And that was when you felt useless. But it was all the same anyway, that's what I figured. Not that I was trying to justify myself or anything . . . and I was never *that* bad anyway. It was just that they both came from the same stirring, to drink or not. I used to think about my father's family and the way he talked about them. They wouldn't have touched a drop, not if their lives depended on it. But I reckon it was the same temptation making us crazy all along. They gave in to fear, I was embracing desire. And they *were* crazy, that's for sure. He chuckles to himself. Did you hear of the monk who spent forty years sitting on top of a column? That was my father's father. And what good did that do him, do you think, except make him all the more crazy for when he finally met his Saviour? And I bet his body was just as ravaged by the end. I mean, wasn't he going to be saved regardless? Why give them the satisfaction, that's what I say, when life does a good enough job on you anyway.

He fluffs his next shot, launching a meaty divot down the fairway instead. He smacks the back of his club into the ground. Nothing is constant, he thinks, not even my fucking golf. And, like that, he wants to win again.

§

They play out thirteen and fourteen in silence and Bill claws a few holes back. On the fifteenth tee Harry feels the need to point out the trees on the right, towards which Bill, with the honour, duly sends his ball. He regrets saying it instantly and is glad to see the ball come up a few yards short of the woods. He consoles himself by telling a story about a man who used to come to the driving range, out by Hadley Airport, who could only hit the ball properly when he insulted it, squeezing out curses the very instant the clubhead made contact. As soon as he tried not to, he forgot how to swing. But he was a bachelor, Harry says, as if by way of explanation, that was the funniest thing. I never knew him with a woman.

He feels again, as soon as the words have remade themselves in silence, that he's said too much, or that he's speaking, rather, as though to take part in some kind of performance. He wonders, in a flash, what it might take to turn his words into poems, then picks up his head to watch Bill walking off in search of his ball, swiping at the long grass with an iron.

He can feel the sweat under his arms when next he swings, his action reverting to a more or less hopeful lunge. His hands are grubby from the grips on the clubs and strafed with thin, rubbery worms which seem to brood in the folds of his palms.

§

They come finally to the eighteenth and walk up and over a low brow, to be rewarded for their exertions with a view of the ocean, vast and old before them. Hitting home. Harry leathers one, catching it just right at last and, for a long few seconds, his ball seems to bob on the distant waves. He can't make them out exactly but the ball's trajectory, coming up to the apex, seems to produce in the blackening blue a wavering that is almost audible, like the static hum of mirage. Another plane overhead, the sun behind them now, going down.

His ball on its way down too, splitting the fairway, Harry's eyes fix on the clubhouse. Again, he sees it as he might a big old family home. There is a narrow road winding down to the front door, lined on one side with poplars. The building in his mind has pointed gables and eaves and wild meadow grass all around. He imagines a wide hallway, with a hatstand, and light streaming through tall windows either side of a heavy door. In an adjacent room, there is a company in full swing, their chatter a dull murmur which papers the thick walls before blaring up when he opens the door.

He wonders if he's imagining a house in Wales, one his father might have seen or known before he left for America, to look for a pious land and end up in Philly. He tries to remember specific stories, from his childhood, and details beyond the imagined or presumed, then realises with a shudder that there aren't any. All of that, the distant past, is a blank; a space that exists in his mind – which he can feel, quite clearly – but whose substance has been used up. As though the stories – even in broad form, the last rumours of their attachment – have simply evaporated.

He tries to console himself with New Jersey – Dunellen, for example, when Mary worked at the asbestos plant and he came along to extract her – but even that seems pale. Nothing but trails of burnt kerosene which you kept looking at, even when they'd dissipated and all there was any more was blue.

They finish up on the green and Harry makes a nice tap-in par. Then they settle up. It crosses his mind that he shouldn't be taking money off his son but at the same time has a vision of them standing there, Harry Leon, in Florida, with his boy of thirty-something. Shaking his hand and thanking him for the game. Call it a dollar, he says.

Bill rummages around in his back pocket for a while before coming up with the note. It has been twice folded – once, crisply, in half, then once over again diagonally in his trousers. Harry takes it off him and, without unfolding the crease, pockets it quickly.

Walking off the course, he says to Bill, What was I saying? Ah yes, I remember. I'm a petty man. I have to take it seriously. And I might be seventy now but I can still hit a ball. The words feel like they ought to be accompanied by a laugh and Bill looks up suddenly. Of course, he says, happy birthday, I'm sorry. He even looks it and Harry notices a dilation in his pupils like the sudden awareness of pain. He gives him a smile, as though to free him of the obligation, and Bill's eyes revert immediately to the floor. Don't worry, Harry says, I was only joking. That's one score I won't be counting any more.

ALL BLUE

They spend the early part of August in the garden, on slow bake. Days pass neither slowly nor quickly, which is to say that there are plenty of occasions on any given day for Harry to wonder what it is he's actually doing to help the sun on its daily pass from red to gold, east to west, but plenty of instances too of him going about his particular nothings only to stop suddenly in the realisation that the swirl of hair they have at the crown, father and son alike, is no longer singeing and that it is already late afternoon or early evening indeed. And from there, the rest of the day is a slow ballad and time itself – without their noticing particularly – has taken on a nondescript quality, as though deprived suddenly of its bite. It is what it is, no more no less, and they – Bill, Mary and him – what *they* are in its default embrace.

Despite being present for the most part in Harry's day, Bill keeps his own hours too. Every few nights or so, after dinner, he leaves the house – to walk around ostensibly and get some cool air, or he goes to a bar, maybe, to sit at the counter quietly for an hour or so and catch whatever he can of that evening's game on a high-perched television. Or out dancing. Whatever it is young people do these days, Harry thinks goofily, slumped by then in his chair. Mary and he are already in bed – and asleep more often than not – by the time he gets back. One night, in the early hours, Harry awakes with a start to the sound of a chair in the kitchen being kicked or leaned into hard, screeching like a jay against the tiled floor.

Come mid-morning, though, without fail, Bill has taken up his place on the bench, where he sits leaning forward, looking out over the rims of his glasses. Every so often, Mary brings him tea, carrying out his mug and the sugar bowl on a tray wide enough for a silver service. Bill's expression remains more or less unchanged throughout the day. Like some television intellectual, Harry thinks, forced to take a holiday but unable still to rid himself of the serious face. If he is down at the bottom end of the garden when Bill makes his appearance – it makes their little plot sound immense – he raises a hand in acknowledgement, man to man.

They eat lunch outside most days, which feels like another contribution to the loosening up of time. And this pleases Mary too, quite obviously – a depthful stir to which Harry isn't party. She can't quite allow herself to relax, though, or even to sit back in her plastic chair while the sun might be capable of soldering leftover sauce onto their plates.

Most of their neighbours, retired like them, those who might be tempted otherwise to look in or down on them as they go about their leisure, seem to be away – taking breaks from their own, perhaps – and what they have, all of a sudden, Harry thinks, what they've done, the three of them, just by sitting there and talking when they have something to say, is stumble upon an idyll. Without even trying – which is either particularly fortunate or particularly galling given that when he did try, it was nothing at all like this.

After a while, Mary, still agitated, can no longer bear the weight of her stillness. She gets up to clear the table but Harry tells her to take it easy. Plenty of time for all that. Which there is now, it would seem. What's more, Bill agrees. Relax, Mom, he says, and Harry raises his eyebrows at his wife, as though to take for granted the camaraderie with their son. Mary acquiesces – to Bill, Harry thinks, not to him – then looks at them both in turn, smiling. And so they go on sitting there, shaded from the Florida sun by a patched-up but still perfectly serviceable parasol that Harry brought home with him from the driving range the week they cleared the place out.

§

Bill and he play golf once, sometimes twice, a week. They try out different courses in the area, interspersing their games with trips down to the range to hone their technique. Harry's requires infinitely more honing than Bill's, who seems to have rediscovered the easy action – hallmark of young learning – which allowed Harry to dream briefly of being kept in the manner to which he'd very quickly become accustomed. He wouldn't have had any qualms, he thinks, about taking the handouts when they came. It wouldn't be like he hadn't played his part. That said, he'd have drunk himself stupid by now, so it was probably for the best . . .

Down on the range they get a big basketful of balls each and stand in adjacent bays, trying to whack the vulcanised orbs into the ocean. The range itself has something of the lookout post about it – corrugated iron huts sat atop a low promontory. Jet trails strafe the sky overhead and every so often, the sheet-metal birds themselves emerge above them, out of the overhanging roof, as though to be picked out of the sky by their highest, proudest drives. They even go down there after dinner one evening, staying late, and hitting then into a floodlit netherworld.

Bill doesn't seem displeased by the activity – which Harry counts both as progress in absolute terms and evidence of the efficacy of his plan. And the afternoons keep on coming, Tuesday's no different from Thursday's or Sunday's. They get their wedges out in the garden too and spend hours here and there chipping from outside the door down to the bottom of the garden and back again. They take small chunks out of the lawn or leave swishy indentations behind them, scraping off just enough of the crispened growth to reveal half-shoots in baby green.

§

One such afternoon, Mary brings out 'lemonade for the workers', on the same silver-service tray used for the tea. She too seems to have perked up in the course of Bill's stay. She is more present suddenly, comes out to the garden a few times during the day and stays, sometimes exchanging just a few words with the sitting idol on her bench, at others staying long enough to engage him in something more like conversation. They look funny sitting there together; Bill is far taller than she is but seems folded in on himself while Mary sits as she has ever since Harry has known her, straight-up orthodox. The difference in size between them isn't immediately obvious.

Bill and Harry approach the table where Mary has set down the tray and prop their clubs against the back of a chair. They stand as she serves them the lemonade from a tall glass jug, in which squeezed-out lemon quarters bob half an inch or so below the surface. When she pours, the sound is full and glugular, rounding off against the deep walls of the glasses. She invites them to add sugar if they need to, which Harry, sitting down, does immediately. He stirs the mixture purposefully then lifts the glass to his lips. He lets out a gasp as the tartness registers on his tongue. Oof, good, he says to Bill, that'll do it.

Sitting down himself now, Bill lifts the glass off the table and leans into it to take a sip off the top. Sugar? Mary asks, concerned. Oh no, thanks, Bill says, it's great like that. Thank you. Mary smiles.

Harry, looking on, catches something in his wife's regard which makes him feel, in an instant, both glad for her and sad. The deep stirring . . . An image from the early days of their marriage comes into his head. Buying milk and eggs on his way home from work with which Mary would make them pancakes. Ordinary feast days, before they had the boys.

They're old now, he thinks. Mary looks old; the whole of her face wrinkles up with her smile. As his must too, he being older still and having been licentious enough in his time for the two of them together. It isn't a realisation, however, more like catching up with an evidence. Something he's known well enough for some years already, having seen the decline as it was happening. He didn't always pay it particular attention but there it was all the same, in the way everything remade itself as present, in flickering permanence, like television. It was the very real evidence of nothing being actually past. Mary's smile, his hands. What he sees now, all he has before him, is everything he's ever seen. Before going to meet Mary, he used to scrub his hands with wire wool, inspecting them carefully for signs of manual labour, then thrust them into his jacket pockets. Twenty-five years later, they'd be swollen and hot when he woke up on mornings after nights before. And all this is perfectly visible, he thinks, in the fact that now they tremble.

§

In front of the television, during the evenings, Harry listens attentively to the sports round-up – a habit of his working life, so that he'd be properly informed for conversations at work. The Yankees are having a rare old summer and every time they see images of Yankee Stadium he turns to Bill and says, Look, there's Harry, right there. To which Bill nods and sort of half smiles. During live games, however, having never been particularly taken by baseball, he watches more for the rhythm of it: whole minutes in which signs are given, calls made and unmade, chewing, spitting, passing the ball from glove to hand to glove to hand. Then the flurry – the pitcher uncoiling as though in some religious rite and minion men dispatched to left-field and right. The dispassionate regard Harry has – not for the players but as though for the game itself and its observances – brings with it the growing sense of being wise to time's little ruses. I see you, boy, he says under his breath, as the picture changes to reveal the pitcher's hands in close-up, I see you.

It is during one of these interludes, however, that he decides. Keeping Bill covered is all very well and good; talking on his behalf he could keep doing until New Jersey won the pennant. But they need decisive action; someone has to toss it up, get the ball in the air again, or else . . . well, kill or cure, he thinks.

He lets it all settle for one whole night then a morning and an afternoon. Before dinner, full of the day's sweat and stick, he spends longer than usual washing his hands, letting them luxuriate in the fountainous spray of cold water – and the relief in his body associates itself with a washing away of something else too, in Bill and him or perhaps in himself only. Then, over dinner, he announces that they'll go down to the bar on Thursday evening for drinks and a bit of a singsong. Mary and Bill respond entirely as expected. They don't say anything but give him their most fervid looks. Mary's is concerned and what are you doing, Bill's almost a perfect void in its expression of mute panic.

§

For as well as talk, Harry sings. It used to be a regular thing – an outing, once-a-week-sacred – and he missed that too when first they moved down the coast. He taught their little band – an Englishman, an Irishman and a Welshman, amongst others – to sing 'Guide Me, O Thou Great Jehovah', on the pretext that it was in *How Green Was My Valley*. And they ended up singing it really rather well, in four more or less defined voices.

With that hard core – men who strike him now as the closest thing he had in his adult life to friends – they reminisced about places and faces of yore. The Irishman was from Cork, born in New York, but spent most of his life in Dunellen. He ran whiskey in the twenties, made a trip over to Queens once a week, then branched out into wholesaling. The Englishman was from Leeds via Jersey City. Harry had never been to either distant town and, more than that, wasn't even sure of being able to pronounce the name of the place where his family came from. Still they spent their evenings singing and talking out old times, compositing their disparate histories onto common ground. They talked themselves as they did so as though into a state of emigration. The old country was gone forever or, more dolorous than that, could no longer be for them. But, while they were able to wallow in its pity . . . They got drunk and felt warm and welcome only to feel too, sometimes even before they arrived home and lurched into sleep but certainly the next morning, creeping shame; that reminiscing about that which they'd never actually been, or rather that which they'd become none-theless, if only in the eyes of others – the Englishman, the Irishman and the Welshman – was no less than total betrayal. They didn't see each other after that, not until the next time, but during the absence felt – it was what Harry felt, in any case – more Welsh than ever, more foreign to it all too, like a country unto himself that had territory nowhere he knew and dates and glories to be marked *in absentia*.

§

They walk down to the bar with their jackets on their arms, hands in trouser pockets. It is nearly eight o'clock and Bill hasn't said a word in hours. Mary cooked them an early dinner, which Harry wolfed down and Bill barely touched. When Bill put on his jacket on the way out of the door – taking it off again just as quickly in the heat – he might have been pulling on chain mail.

Even Harry is quiet now, though, nervous suddenly, and they walk to the same rhythm, slowly, only picking it up slightly when they get to the last corner of their estate and come across a man slumped against the protective shutter of a liquor store shouting to himself in Spanish.

When they are out of earshot again, Harry realises that the streets around are unusually calm. The traffic is barely a trickle and the grumble of engines, so thick and phlegmy as a rule, is disarmingly distant. They can hear birdsong too, coming down at them from the roofs to set the evening atwitter.

Rounding the corner and arriving at last at the bar, they are met by the roar of a motorbike. It breaks out like thunder and Harry stops in front of the door to compose himself. He holds the door open for Bill but ends up going through it himself, when his son shows no sign of advancing.

Inside, he looks around the room and says Evening to the few patrons sat at the bar or in a small group a little more than halfway along the narrow room. He turns back on himself to hang up his jacket on a peg between the end of the bar and the glass frontage, holding out his hand to take Bill's too. Who is still standing in the open doorway and looking as thoroughly out of place as a man could be. You wouldn't say that he spent his life hanging around bars and clubs, Harry thinks. They pull themselves up onto two stools and spend a few seconds squirming as they try to fit their legs into a space that doesn't really exist.

The barman – a man in his fifties and a stained apron – is upon them immediately. Hello Harry, what'll it be, he says, looking at Bill. Couple of beers, Harry says. Thirsty work, eh, he says then, as the barman turns his back on them and bends towards the fridge. Having plonked their bottles on the metal bar in front of them, Harry's frothing up vigorously, the barman returns to his position roughly equidistant from all the customers – some ten or twelve in all – not talking to any but not ignoring them either. Just like in Plainfield, Harry thinks, where the owner managed to greet his customers with something like feigned familiarity even when they'd been going there at least once a week for, what was it, twenty-odd years by the end. It didn't matter so much there, though, and Harry even enjoyed the provocation. Evans, he'd say, Harry, delighted, every time he shook the man's hand.

Harry looks around now as though for inspiration or distraction, aware suddenly of the quiet beside him. How odd must they look, sitting there not saying a word. Nobody is paying them the slightest attention, however, and Harry notices two of his acquaintances sitting at one of the tables. Both retired mechanics – one facing him but engaged in conversation with the other who is recognisable by the curve of his spine. The former looks up, eventually, and mouths a silent greeting, causing the other to look round too. Harry, he says, how do. We singing tonight? Harry takes a big gulp of beer then says, I'll be singing. I don't know about you lot. I've heard crows with nicer voices.

This is Billy, he says, now that he has their attention, my boy. He's staying with us for a while. Down from New York.

Vacation, eh, the second man says, a Bill too as it happens. Bit of Florida sun. Nice. Nice to meet you. Bill nods in their direction, friendly and accepting, but doesn't say anything. Harry is about to tell them that his son is a musician, a pianist, but his eyes fall on the old upright pushed up against the back wall, piled up with magazines and crockery, and he bites his tongue.

§

Instead, he finishes his beer and gestures to the barman for another. Just one, he says, when he sees him reaching into the fridge for a second. Bill lifts his bottle to his lips and takes two small sips, wetting his lips as though to show willing. Remember when you were young? Harry says, looking down at the counter like Bill and speaking quietly. There was always music. When we went over to the Epps' or when the boys came over. Somebody was always singing or going to the piano to play something. It was nice. You remember? Bill rearranges his beer on the counter, moving it out of the rings of moisture that have formed at the bottom of the bottle. Long time ago, he says. Harry lifts his bottle by the neck, between his thumb and index finger, and gently taps the bottom of Bill's.

You used to come in with us sometimes, when we sang.

You remember? You and Harry. I'd come into the kitchen to get you, but you were always waiting at the door anyway. Like all you wanted was to join us. Your mother didn't like that. She must have thought we'd be a bad influence. But you played for us, pieces you'd learned that week or tunes you'd already memorised. We had to persuade you – you more than Harry – but you always played. And when everybody cheered at the end you loved it. You remember? Your first regular gig.

Harry smiles and drinks some beer.

After Bill's recitals, he usually sang himself. He stood tall, with a hand on Bill's shoulder – Harry's too – and belted out the only song in Welsh he could still remember from his youth. Long forgotten now. His pronunciation even then was probably terrible but nobody'd be any the wiser, not even Paddy. He sang with something like affectation, he remembers, a tenor that was unfamiliar even beyond the strangeness of the words. Or was it rather not affectation at all but some swollen strains of devotion? It sometimes happened that he could hear himself singing, as if from the outside. That was a funny feeling. And when he finished, the others got to their feet and gave him a cheer too, glasses raised high to the heavens, mocking him gently.

§

His second beer halfway down, Harry is already thinking about the next. Through the brown glass is the old feeling – for life effervescent. Or else the bubbles are memory itself, expiring in explosions proper to their size and vigour when they get to the top. Either way, it is a craving for company, to be taken out of himself and forgotten, if only for the evening.

He needs to get them going, he thinks, but registers at the same time a twinge of resentment. Why should he always be the one? He drains the rest of his beer, signalling with his free hand for another. Waving a couple of fingers in Bill's direction too. He takes the bottle from his lips and says to the barman, Put a couple of small ones next to them. Then he calls out to the other Bill, and to Dick sitting opposite him. Hey, what about it? What about what? 'Oh When the Saints'. Bit early yet, Dick says, we still need anointing.

§

In the course of the evening, Harry and Bill move over to sit with the others at the table. Bill responds politely to their questions – about New York, mainly, or if he knew Bird – and Harry wonders what it is about the questions of strangers, as opposed to those of nearest and dearest, that won't allow them to go unanswered.

A few drinks in, he is less inclined to humour the

straggling band but he marches them all the same, militarily, through a few oldies. 'Sweet Georgia Brown' and 'Danny Boy'. Driving them in song and in drink. The energy seems born of the need to keep Bill entertained – or to ensure that the evening will pass for memorable when he is able to reflect on it later. More than that, though, it is as if Harry needs Bill to see him in a company of men. Something about his uncontrollable self running away with him . . . He catches himself at one point teasing the barman about his apron and is embarrassed, as if he had no idea why he might be speaking the words.

The singing that evening is substandard, which Harry feels is as much his fault as anybody else's. He can hear an old-man vibrato in his long notes, of the kind that always made him think affectionately of older acquaintance when he was younger but which, in himself, is nothing short of affliction, desolation. He remembers the impression he used to get back in New Jersey, when their little group sang well, of a direct link between tonality and happiness, which was perhaps not a link at all but an awareness, occasioned by the music, of the very location of happiness. When their voices came together everything did, in good sense and order. Now, he can no more hold a note than he can . . . but he's still standing.

§

Their choir disperses after a few more abortive attempts into chatter and fuzz. The other Bill and Dick go to the bathroom one after the other and stand at the bar when they come back, to drink amongst themselves. The others, who have arrived in the course of the evening and can usually be relied upon to provide encouragement – even if their singing itself is at best uncultured – are half-hearted this evening, standing between the bar and the table and dropping out mid-verse as they please.

Bill's bottle has been empty for at least twenty minutes as Harry spends interludes now looking intently at the table, his eyes full of contemplative steel. Staring into his own bottle or swilling the whiskey he's ordered around in its glass as if it were vital force. He looks over his shoulder occasionally, to bark reproaches or annoyances at whoever is there to hear them. The words are mouthed more than voiced though and, when he turns back to his beer, frustration progressing with incurable logic into melancholy, he looks spent, as though the emissions were the last remnants of a life lived louder. He springs up from his seat after a while and, in the same movement, squeezes into the free space at the bar to order two more beers and two more whiskies. It is difficult to say whether the lunge is deliberately executed or a happy accident. The barman, in any case, lays the drinks out on the counter at which point Harry lumbers off to the toilet, holding his hands out in front of him, in preparation for any unforeseen falling off of the floor.

As he walks back to the table, Bill is looking up at last, at the piano and into the corner of the room where the mirror on the side wall meets the ceiling. Harry sits down and starts to talk, leaning forward to prop his head on his right hand. In real proximity to Bill albeit looking away from him.

I put your mother through a lot, you know, back in the day. She's a good woman and I put her through a lot. You wouldn't have noticed it, Harry and you, you were only kids, but, well, there you go.

He pauses for a moment, during which time Bill repositions himself in his seat. Harry is still sharp enough to take the movement for apprehension and he begins again immediately.

It was the music, you know? It was all about the music. But we took advantage. We had a real nice group back then. There were five or six of us and we sang well together. Even if I say so myself. He pivots his arm so that his head turns in Bill's direction – enough only for him to see folds at the thigh in his flannel trousers. We used to go down to the bar in town and to each other's houses too. Thursdays. You probably don't remember. They lived all over. Sometimes we'd be out in Manville, sometimes in Dunellen but it was our house mostly. We always drank too much – but we sang well. Not like tonight. My Irish friend had a lovely bass, you'd have to say that. We took advantage. I stayed out all night sometimes. You probably don't remember. But I was always back in time for breakfast. You'd be getting ready for school upstairs. Then you'd come down for breakfast and I'd ruffle your hair. Harry stops suddenly. And your mother, bless her, she always had breakfast ready for us. She was good as gold, all along.

§

There is only one place left to go all of a sudden and Harry orders himself another whiskey. And a beer for Bill. All the way to the end. He isn't so stable any more and his long face, given respectability down the years by a nose that ran almost the entire length of it, is slumping at the jowls, the weight in his head pushing down into bands of flesh that lavish at the neck. The vapour blue in his eyes is evaporating fast. But he still has the memory, in his body and in his being, of abuses past – a force that won't allow itself to be exhausted – and he raises his head to look into Bill's eyes. Bill looks back at him, lifting his bottle to take a modest glug this time. He purses his lips as he puts it down again, in the guise of a smile perhaps.

I wouldn't have done anything differently, Harry says, if I had my time back. I don't think I could have. But his voice is viscous now. You can't help yourself half the time and the other half there's no choice. You have to work. You have to. And then one day you look around you and you see people, you look them up and down, in the mirror too, and you think, Ah, he was successful, he retired to Florida. He had a couple of businesses in New Jersey. Ordinary enough – but he took his chances. And now he's happy. Good for him. But you never know, do you, how much it costs. What it actually costs. You only work it out later. That all the successes you came by, you paid for them dearly, in fact. With all the little disappointments along the way. Nothing is what you wanted it to be, is it. Not really, I mean. It always looks a bit different to how you imagined. He has a pause for thought, during which the decades seem to slide – vast continental slabs, of ice or rock, breaking up slowly in a blue-grey flow. The thirties, the forties, the fifties – and now the nineteen sixties. A long old time.

§

The room has emptied around them and the barman is going around the tables collecting glasses on a star-spangled melamine tray. He takes them back behind the bar and places them one at a time into the sink. After wiping down the counter, starting by the window and working his way back, he comes over to the table and says to the back of Harry's head that he'll call them a taxi. Bill nods.

They don't say a word on their way out. Bill pushes back his chair and there is a shriek in anguish as the metal scuffs the tiles. Harry clasps the sides of the table to push himself onto his feet. They walk towards the door in line abreast, Harry leaning ever so slightly into his son. Bill opens the door for him and Harry goes through, placing a hand on the window for support as soon as he is outside. Then Bill turns around and raises his hand at the barman, who does likewise, already moving in their direction to bolt the door.

They stand in silence for a few minutes, waiting for the taxi. Harry blows out a couple of deep breaths and Bill puts his hands in his trouser pockets, taking them out again when the barman opens the door behind them to hand them the jackets that they've forgotten. Thank you.

The taxi arrives and they climb into the back, Bill roadside. Harry blurts out their address and they set off, through traffic lights that are just turning red. Harry opens his window an inch or so and lifts his forehead into the draught. The beads of sweat on his hairline are crystallising hard. He looks over at Bill and can barely make him out in profile, angled out of the streetlights. He thinks again about speaking – torrents of interference – and of a more pressing need now to communicate, any which way, into silence.

At home, they switch on the light in the hallway but leave the kitchen lights off. Harry pours them a glass of water each from the tap, which they drink standing a couple of feet apart. Then he bids Bill goodnight and goes upstairs, gripping the banister tight.

IN BLACK AND WHITE

They settle into a period of calm. Harry doesn't talk too much but doesn't think too much either, as though his hangover of the following morning – a slow emptiness interspersed with faint trembling in his calves – had set in for good. The weather stays hot and muggy but he seems to be bearing it better suddenly. Not that he wouldn't quite happily take a few days of respite. Out in the garden, looking over the roof of the house into the permanent blue, he remembers the summer storms that flared up in New Jersey, as soon as they had three straight days of sun. They subsided just as quickly but left everything rain-fresh and good. Learning to live without it, Harry thinks, not to fight it any more, but what 'it' might be he doesn't even stop to consider.

Mary maintains a serene complexion as well. She seems more content in domesticity than Harry can ever recall seeing her. She goes to bed early, gets up a little later than before and sleeps right through, which he has occasion to notice when his bladder delays his passage into sleep and hastens his coming to.

And then there is Bill, for whom home seems to be doing its work. Not unequivocally, perhaps, not yet, but his silence no longer seems to carry in it the imminent threat of melt-down. And his parents are better able to bear it. Harry still sees more of him than Mary, out in the garden, but for now at least there is more cause to worry about the state of the lawn than about the state of Bill's mind, and that can only be a good thing.

They might have carried on like that in perpetuity, Harry thinks, until the transformation was complete and they hadn't even noticed, had not the post brought, one morning, a letter from New York. It is a request for Bill to write liner notes for his forthcoming album – the selection of record-ings from his concerts with Scott LaFaro that they're rushing out for September, while death is still the order of the day.

Mary and Harry only learn all that later, though. As soon as Bill reads the letter, not even running to a whole page and whose black hand Harry can make out through the thin paper, the quiet falls upon him again, forbidding like before. They understand, at the very least, that it isn't news to fill a wounded heart with joy. And then he is gone, as soon as he can politely finish his breakfast and make his excuses. Out to get some fresh air.

He doesn't return until early evening but neither Mary

nor Harry question him about his day. Neither do they need to, for he comes back in surprisingly fine fettle. In the living room, he tells his father, of his own volition, about the letter and Harry feels as though his son is actively seeking his counsel. He is under pressure, suddenly, as if all his talk of the past few weeks has had this in mind the whole time. He hears himself mumbling then remembers the feeling he had, when Bill had just arrived, of acquiring wisdom. People want you to be things, Harry says. They all want something from you, don't they. His tone is questioning, though, as if it were his turn now to seek Bill's accord. They can't help it but they expect all the same – and that's what gets you. Neither a borrower nor a lender be, that's what I say. Behind his glasses, Bill has a kindly look in his eyes. And what's worse, Harry says, emboldened, is when they want to help you, or when they say it'll do you good. I always hated that the most.

§

Harry and Mary retire early that evening – a little too early to be going to bed but they go all the same, united in their appreciation of the need to give Billy some space. If Bill himself is wise to the ruse, he doesn't let on. They sit up reading for a while, Mary flicking distractedly through a magazine, Harry reading the day's paper. They are both, he realises, some minutes in, listening more than they are reading, as though waiting for something external to lead them out of the impasse. Nothing is forthcoming, though, and before long they place their reading material on their respective bedside tables and switch off the lamps.

No sooner have they done so than they hear the piano in the living room beneath them. The deeper notes seem to emanate as though from the wall behind the headboard. Harry feels Mary's body freezing, a tremor in the mattress, and stays stock still himself until the pressure on his elbow is too great. Letting his weight release into his back, he has an impression of it being dark in the living room too.

The song is a slow ballad, hitherto unknown to Harry, and Bill is obviously playing as quietly as he can. The notes ring out all the same – albeit at some unfathomable distance, like pebbles dropping into a deep well. Mary whispers something that he doesn't quite catch but he doesn't ask her to repeat it, preferring to lie still, not even to open his mouth.

When the song comes to an end, Harry turns to face Mary who is facing him now too and they stay like that for a few moments, unable to see each other, until it is obvious that Bill has finished playing.

§

More calm then. Days of sun and quiet, until a week or two later when the US Mail comes once again to the fore, delivering in time for Bill's birthday an advance copy of the record. Bill hands it round at the breakfast table, blushing to the base of his ears, for Mary first then Harry to look at. Harry reads the words carefully. Bill Evans Trio, *Sunday at the Village Vanguard*, featuring Scott LaFaro. On the cover, Bill looks only just warm, like the fulfilment of premonition. Only half his face is visible, one eye peering reluctantly into the lens, as though obliged to take in the light, while the other takes refuge in pushed contrast. His hands have a certain prominence but only two fingers on his left hand, cigarette wedged between them, and the index finger of the right are extended. It looks like he has some treasured possession in his balled palms which he wants to keep for himself.

On the back cover are the liner notes Bill never wrote – a dozen or so paragraphs that recount, by omission, his summer in black and white. And more too, Harry thinks, a greater, wider narrative; something hidden and true that they will have known, the three of them together, one and one and one.

§

Mary cooks a birthday chicken in the evening and they sit down to eat, full of respect for the occasion. Harry goes easy on the ketchup and chews each mouthful thirty-two times. Delicious, delicious, he says, and the eating is indeed happy when they dispense with the ceremony and tuck in. Bill seems particularly pleased with his chicken.

After dinner, in the sitting room, Harry puts on Bill's record, and Bill reacts this time with equanimity. They hear the song he played in the living room – it's called 'My Man's Gone Now' – and Harry and Mary exchange shadowy glances. The recording is peppered with audience participation. Little hints of conversation, applause blurted out into the hanging calm at the end of songs and the clinking of glasses. Harry listens for these particularly. They make him feel by turns sad and wistful and glad – or else just thirsty.

But he reacts to the music too, feeling for once that he can let himself be guided by his own sense of its unfolding. He hears in Bill's licks and loops the phrasing of something familiar and logical, as if it were the playing out of his own enigma. He nods in appreciation then looks up. It transpires that he is reacting with Bill himself. They come together in nods and rueful smiles.

Harry feels sure that Bill knows the exact reasons for his wonderment – be they triads or tenths or whatever – and it occurs to him that his son might be pitying him or, at the very least, humouring the old man in his incomprehension. He lets the thought extend to wonder whether it wasn't pity, finally, that joined him to his wife, when it flattered him to think that he could save her. Her dead father and dead-end job. His intentions were more noble than that, more decent – but they were pitiful nonetheless. And maybe that was what enabled them to make it so far together, down the long Route 1.

He looks up again from the music and there is Bill unhappy now. Harry feels it too. Sad like the sadness that won't bear discussion, that won't even bear recognition. He ventures a smile, of mutual encouragement, but Bill looks away immediately.

Harry imagines his son back in New York and going out on the road. Driving, or being driven around, and pulling up to junctions and traffic lights on the outskirts of a city. As far away from them by then, Mary and him and home, as if they'd simply, gently, dropped out of existence.

The recording lasts some forty minutes. As it comes to an end, Harry pours himself a whiskey from the cabinet. A last one, he thinks, to mark the occasion. Bill has got a hold of himself again now and he accepts the offer too, quite willingly. He stands up to receive his glass and, as the needle on the record player slides into the empty groove, they clink. That's life imitating art, Harry says, right there. Good health. Long life.

§

One morning shortly after that, Harry goes into the kitchen and hears Mary on the phone with Jr in New York. She lowers her voice when she hears him approaching then looks around to check. Harry points to the garden behind him with his thumb. He'll be back end of the week, Mary says into the receiver, almost whispering. He's OK, yes, he's OK. But keep an eye on him if you can, for me.

Then the day itself arrives, breaking with humid indifference. They try to follow suit, not to make of it any more than is absolutely necessary. Mary busies around the place, checking and double-checking the laundry basket, and Harry goes into the garden for an hour or two. He and Bill hit a few balls together. Goodbye is a handshake and a hug after lunch.

In the car on the way to the airport, they hear on the radio that Hurricane Carla has hit Texas, killing some dozens of people at least. It takes the peripheral rains until early evening to reach Florida.

ACKNOWLEDGEMENT
[BILL]

DA CAPO

Filling up with deep reckoning on the approach into Newark Metropolitan. Dipping violently out of dragon-breath clouds, the descent cushioned only by occasional swells and updrafts. When the city comes into view, nothing looks particularly high and even the Empire State Building is no more than another pine in the island forest. Bill tries to bring to mind the view in reverse, when he stops in the street and tilts back his head for the metal trunks to communicate down from the heavens rather than up into man's ambition. The plane banks right, as though to dive headlong into the city and, in the breathlessness of freefall, he has a feeling for the transubstantiation by which he will have been made, before dark, to walk again in the city's cadence.

As they come out of the dive, the cabin fills by degrees with the red augur of evening. It splurges first on the plastic roof then on seat-backs and trays, settling finally on faces and hands. The particular tint has about it the lucency of

skin, like heat felt through fine-wrought gauze, and it causes
Bill to think – though only to read, in fact, the evidence of
his eyes – that it is in bright, late bloom that the light goes
out of the world.

§

The principal expression of his discontent is physical for the
time being. At the conveyor belt, waiting to retrieve his bag,
he has half a tune in his head which he can't quite bring to
his lips. He shifts his weight from one leg to the other, as
though to jog the needle out of its groove. Beyond the exit
door, he can imagine Harry waiting for him, walking around
the concourse and picking up a magazine at the newsstand
before putting it down again immediately. But he can't imagine
actually meeting him, greeting him or getting into his car.
And for as long as he has the snippet of melody in his mind
and he can take it only so far without extrapolating or
inventing, it is the expression of a defective mechanics, mind
and body and soul, bound together in hapless unbeknowing.

§

When he emerges at last, through grey-wash double doors,
the press-pack consists of elderly, life-worn parents, taxi
drivers sporting various combinations of jacket and hat, and

the representatives of a trade fair in Jersey City. Their boards and cards bear names in American Polish. Bill meets one or two regards, then lowers his head to plod into the concourse's unfeeling arms. It is fair to say that no one in the waiting throng has paid him all that much attention, except to let disappointment register briefly on their faces when it became apparent that he wasn't their Mr Voychek or Atlantic Plastic from Lakewood.

Nor does Harry make a show of picking out his brother in the crowd. The first notion Bill has of his presence is when he feels someone walking the same step pattern as him, behind his left shoulder. At which point he stops and turns around, his eyes catching his brother's chest first of all and the flannel grey of his jacket. When he looks into Harry's face, he sees the bruised blood vessels around his nose before their eyes come together. Harry's spring to life immediately, whereas Bill's still have about them a sky-high sheen. A flash of fear as well, igniting and snuffing itself out in the same instant.

Hello, Harry says. How was the flight? The car's out front.

§

They walk out of the terminal building into the granular heat of idling engines and spent kerosene. This way, Harry says, and Bill once again looks up from the default head down of his two months away. You didn't need to come and meet me, he replies. I could have made my own way back. Oh sure thing, Harry says at once, it's no bother. Here, let me take that, and he reaches down and across for Bill's brown leather companion, plucking it out of his left hand as though to confiscate it from a naughty child. Sure thing, he says again, walking on and leaving Bill trailing momentarily. Thanks, Bill says, to his brother's back.

Harry turns back towards him after a couple of determined steps and has a look in his eye like he wants to say something funny. He comes to a halt himself. You know, he says, before deciding that he doesn't want to say it after all. How was Florida? Hot I bet. Yeah, and they walk on. We played golf, Bill says. Really? Great! You still tearing it up? I guess. We should try and have a game here, says Harry, radiating enthusiasm, while the weather's still OK. We could even go out to New Jersey. Sure thing, Bill replies, taking up his brother's phrase, not entirely innocently though perhaps not in such a way that it will be taken amiss.

§

He closes his eyes in the car, less out of tiredness than to allow his mind some catch-up time and space. What daylight remains seems quite unforgiving all of a sudden and he prefers to hear the journey unfold in hums and drones more akin to those of his body and his brain ticking over. While they scoot up Route 1, he tunes in to the duh-dump pulse of front and back wheels on the sectioned tarmac, letting the regularity of the motion through the seat rock him gently into rest. When he opens his eyes again, they are on the slip road leading up to the turnpike and, as they nurse the long bend, four or five streetlights move from line abreast into military formation before fanning out again in the opposite direction. Harry is tapping noiselessly at his knee, touching his kneecap with the tip of his middle finger. He reaches forward once in a while to tap at the gearstick too and the movement has something compulsive about it, like drumming, or like the movement brought on by a cold breeze that has already claimed outer layers but won't be content until it has made its way through to the bones.

Bill looks over at his brother, who might or might not be aware of the gaze in his direction. Only when they have safely merged with the faster traffic on the turnpike and are looking to pull back into the slow lane does Harry cast his eyes in Bill's direction, checking through the passenger window and behind Bill's head for anything in his blind spot. They speed their way towards the city, taking it in turns to exchange glances with the drivers of passing cars. Bill looks to his right at those they overtake, Harry left when they in turn are overtaken. The meeting of eyes has something zoological about it, like a scoping out of caged beasts.

§

In Union City they wind their way through underpasses and tunnels, as though to feel in the air about them, or in the rubbing of finger and thumb, the waxy Apple aura. Even when they aren't buried under other roads, or in the shadows of houses built in suspension above them, they are enclosed on either side by sheer walls quarried out of the rock. The inside of the car is thrown into premature dusk and the hastily applied rouge of brake lights smudges itself on the windscreen. They are bumper to bumper now, even if the worst of the traffic is on the other side, heading out to weekends away and the wife.

They can't not speak any longer it seems, and Harry takes the past for his text. How long since we first came this way on the bus? Without Mom, I mean? He sounds like he wants to give an impression of wondering aloud, as though he'd have said the words even without his brother in the car. But Bill, as it happens, isn't unwilling to play along. Oh, long time, he says. Best part of twenty years. Yeah, I guess so, Harry says. You believe that? I was thinking about it the other day. You remember who we saw at the Adams? That's where we saw Bud Powell, right? Or was that in New York?

Probably was, come to think of it. The Three Deuces, right? Right. And those fake draft-cards we had. The guy on yours even had a beard, didn't he? I . . . don't remember, Bill says, redistributing his weight in the seat as though to offset annoyance. Harry lets a few seconds go by. I don't know, he says, to bring them back from the brink of indiscretion. It'd be nice to be able to bunk off again now, eh? Once in a while? When Bill looks over at him, Harry seems troubled, in his brow and around his visible eye. It would, Bill says, and he waits for their eyes to meet to give him a smile.

Then they're moving relatively freely again and approaching the Lincoln Tunnel. After taking it in turns to puff out their cheeks and exhale more or less dramatically, Bill asks Harry how Debby's doing. Oh, she's just fine, he says, adding thanks after a barely perceptible pause.

§

They come up on West 40th, swinging left immediately and round and right onto 10th Avenue. When they get into the 60s, Harry asks if Bill wouldn't prefer to come to their place first, have Pat fix them something to eat, maybe stay the night. Bill thinks about it for a second or so. Thank you, he says, you're kind. But I need to be getting back. No problem, Harry says, but if you ever want to . . . Yes, Bill says. Of course.

They park up outside the apartment block and Harry walks round to get the bag out of the boot. He holds it in his hand while Bill comes back to join him. I can bring this up, he says, hoisting it onto his shoulder. That's OK, Bill says. I'll manage. You've done enough already. It was kind of you to come and get me. Oh, sure thing, says Harry, sure thing.

They shake hands. Say hi to the gang, Bill says as his brother gets back in the car. Will do. Then the door slams shut, the engine starts and Bill slaps the back windscreen twice with his palm.

§

Bill gets into his apartment and slumps back against the closed door, his body free at last to express its exhaustion. Opening his eyes onto an unsent letter, a subway token and a handful of loose change, sitting on the shelf in the hallway, where they were when he left. The sounds too are inconspicuously familiar: the gentle hum of the fridge a few paces away in the kitchen, a creaking in the floorboards at the other end of the corridor, and the bathroom door that moves up and down on its hinges an eighth of an inch or so when the front door closes. The light in the hallway makes the walls seem less white, more yellow and smoky than he remembers but, apart from that, it is as if he'd been there all along – sitting on the sofa or at the piano, waiting to greet his returning alter ego.

He places the meagre accumulation of post from his box downstairs on the shelf, lodging it upright behind the pile of coins, then puts his bag down at his feet. He goes into the kitchen and, without turning on the light, runs the cold-water tap. He takes a mug from the draining board, fills it then drinks it down in one. Back in the hallway, he picks up the pile of post again and walks through to the living room, squeezing around the piano like second nature.

Only when he sits down, keeping a straight back despite the softness of the sofa, does a sense of the oddness come upon him. The light from the table lamp to his right casts out over a thickish layer of dust on the piano lid, revealing a thinner layer too, as perfectly round as the ashtray was when it sat there in vigil for three days and nights.

Most of the envelopes are run of the mill and he throws them onto the other half of the sofa. But there is another, addressed to his better-known self, and he opens this one immediately. Inside the envelope is a single sheet of paper, folded over once then once more, through the back of which he can see a familiar scrawl. The second fold reveals a small wad of banknotes – fives and tens, coming to a hundred, maybe, in all. He leans forward to place the letter on top of the piano but keeps the money in his left hand. Then he gets up from the sofa and, with his right hand, wipes as much dust off the lid as he can. The white keys, exposed again to the lamplight, are oysterous, the black laced with silver where his fingers, for all their apparent glide, have left snail-trail deposits. He puts the money back in the envelope and wedges it between B and C at the bass end. Bills for William and bills for Bill, he thinks, sitting down again.

Between letting go of his weight and feeling it gather up in the cushions, something flips in his mind. He tries to fish out a cigarette from his trouser pocket and has to lift his buttocks off the seat to facilitate the manoeuvre. And he can't find a comfortable position after that. He tries bringing his left leg up under his body, even sitting cross-legged, but to no avail. His cigarette clinging to his bottom lip, he goes back into the hall, to his bag, which he picks up and takes into the bedroom. He places it in the middle of the bed, stubs out his smoke in the ashtray on the bedside table and pulls open the zip with a flourish.

His mother has laid a clean towel, one of her own, over the top of his things and he takes it out and puts it to one side, taking care to preserve the folds. She's also provided him with apples and oranges, a couple of packs of coffee and another oblong packet wrapped in aluminium foil. Its sides have been folded just as carefully as the towel, over and under. He takes it out and unwraps it. There is a further layer, of wax paper, but inside are two lots of two triangular sandwiches, stuffed full of chicken and green leaves.

He is back at once in his army days and the daily round of marches and shouting. Getting back to the base after weekends at home to find bars of chocolate in the folds of his clothes or an ice-cream tub full of Russian salad. To help him, however temporarily, through his displacement. He'd come across the little gifts and spend a while overwhelmed, sitting on the very edge of his bottom bunk. And he owes it to his mother, suddenly, not to be unhappy. He owes it to Mary Soroka, Mary the magpie, whose sharp features he has inherited so well, who worries grievously in any case and if she only knew . . . To his father too, the troubled look in his brother's eyes and the togetherness of their youth. Not to mention to himself, to the child he was in good faith and hope. He thinks of his grandmother, sitting at the kitchen table, topping and tailing string beans, piling them up in a deep ceramic bowl. He wonders if she'd recognise him now. His Billyness, the plainness of his habits and loves – but the vastness of his soul too, pushed so terribly hard.

He gets down off the bed eventually and takes his packet of sandwiches into the living room. He goes to sit at the piano and unwraps the foil over middle C, to eat and let the crumbs fall where they will.

CODA

On his own, detached from the counterpoint of a brother, parents, even a more or less familiar street or city scene. Sitting at the piano, all traces of recent attachment having worn off, Bill is left to contemplate the lacquer and the grain and the ordinary conundrums of an existence in one's head. But it is by no means certain, of course, that he sees either the lacquer or the grain. Or if he does, or if he looks at the keys and registers the polished craft of their construction, it is from a consciousness filtered through his army years, for example, and the period afterwards in particular, when he went back home to Jersey to recuperate from the battering. Days, weeks and months which he spent in isolation, playing himself in and out and around the various modes and keys. Entire mornings voicing the particular tones of his fragility, afternoons running his right hand ragged, as though vindictively, up and down the octaves.

It might have seemed at that time like he was building something substantial; a safe haven, fortified with the materials available to him, against barbarian invasion; the place he'd go to when the time came and whose rooms and halls he decorated over the course of seven subsequent years in studios and back-room bars, in half-light and night shade. To arrive, when his confidence caught up at long last with his ability, at the Vanguard . . .

In the concerted lamplight, a view of him in abstraction suggests itself. The opaque glass of the long window reflects the commanding dark, which is at once the black reflection of the piano and the nowhere recesses of the city beyond. Bill is surrounded by it, above and below as well as on either side. He is still dead centre, hunched over the piano, his head barely visible on his shoulders, but while he remains stranded in still life – and even after that, when a murmur of movement can be discerned in his shoulders – the impression is of a breathing machine built to carry out atavistic orders, to eat and work and dream; and brought to life, furthermore, by a force which cares nothing for the individual blade of grass, only for the entire field.

What he might once have thought of as construction, then, was in fact the effacement of those selfsame structures. What required his time and trance-like devotion, day after night after day, was in fact a whole other system, over whose workings he couldn't have hoped to exercise the least control.

Because what it required of him, precisely, was that he think with his hands, to unoccupy the territory.

For as long as it is dark, then, Bill remains visible. He is certainly a better fit with the relative isolation of a sparsely furnished room than with the bustle of breakfast counters, for example, preachers of doom on 42nd Street or Coke-signed plazas. More than that, though, his pale complexion seems not to need or want or, more correctly perhaps, to trust the light. He is quite exceedingly white – so much so that photographs of him seem more like negatives. His barn-owl face with its black-hole eyes is an image of something getting in the way of the light – that something being his capacity for reflection, precisely. And his sentient being will *always* be in the way, such that he is obliged to experience life from the outside, like looking through thick plate glass. How much he might have liked, for example, to tell Mary that he enjoyed sitting with her in the garden. How well he might have shared with Harry the little of music he knew. What music he might have made himself, or with Scott and Paul.

Bill draws the tip of the middle finger on his right hand down over F sharp into the groove between F and G, repeating the gesture calmly and deliberately. He presses down eventually on the black note to hear its gentle glow. Considering it, feeling it, letting it sing somewhere distant. He gives it a D complement with the middle finger of his left hand and plays the combination a second time, before moving down to F and C sharp.

Even with the musical intervention, though, he will only sit at the piano for so long. The time will come, and soon, when he has to leave the house and get out on the streets. Walk up to Harlem, keep his wits about him, and try to bluff his way through a trade. But he'll get home again, not particularly late, shut the door behind him and breathe in, long and deep, the pre-emptive draw of fulfilment. Then he'll go to the bedside table, where he keeps the needle and the strap, and all of this will go away.

§

When he wakes up the following morning, the bedclothes have been kicked all over the place. He has slept uneasily but can't recall any of the visions that must have agitated him as night turned on to morning.

He has a vehement erection and for a while all his force seems channelled through it. He is lying on his side, on his arm, but hasn't yet registered the discomfort. Then he is lying on his back, his body having taken upon itself the duty of care. Wondrous thing. He thinks about the hormones it sent flowing this way and that, the hair it sprouted and the thumbs that doubled in size. All while he wasn't looking. And even though he can remember a time when his reach was barely six notes, how tame the whole process was. It should have provoked in him so much more than the odd adolescent glitch.

He feels his heart beating and a second, lighter pulse in his penis. He realises, almost mechanically, that he is contemplating some part of the deeper, oblique self that he only seems to get close to otherwise when he is high. It is a feeling for the non-exclusivity of growth and degradation, of something soaring. It should all go wrong at the drop of a hat, *we* should go wrong – yet men and women endure.

He is looking through his eyes when next he registers his awareness. A small black circle has taken up residence in his vision – an aberration on his retina or some other minor blemish. It resembles a rangefinder or a focus ring in miniature and falls lazily through his vision, as though to draw arcs in feathered felt pen the length and breadth of the bedroom wall. He wonders if it is meant to be there, given that he has never noticed it before, and tries to get a good look at it. Wherever he focuses, though, the mark has already been and gone.

He thinks about getting up but rejects the idea instantly. He wants to keep the outside world at bay for as long as possible. And it isn't like he couldn't sleep another hour or so easily enough. He thinks about acquaintance and obligation, the people who'll come to make sure that he's all right, offer to make him food or coffee or just to sit with him for half an hour. They'll be visiting to give their own sadness an outing too, perhaps, curious to see how much more it affects him, to have lost his right hand. Even though he's left-handed. It won't mean that they aren't genuinely concerned – and they will all have been good enough to him besides, over the years, to be quite legitimate participants. Maybe, simply enough, it's like Harry Sr said. They all want something from you. They can't help it.

He does get out of bed eventually, to stand about in the kitchen. Drinking his mother's coffee then washing the cup and wiping down the worktops and the insides of the sink. He opens the small square window and stands with his right eye to the vertical slit, looking out over air ducts and fire escapes as though through a rip in the decor. After a while, he goes into the living room and opens the window there. When he leans out, he can see the trees in the park at the end of the street. His impression is of a world beyond the stage, a place where the air is cold but where the sun nevertheless carves out long, meticulous shadows.

AL FINE

By the onset of winter he is back, in certain respects, on the grid. He has already played a few dates, solo, and even sat in on a recording, filling the chair at the last minute to provide accompaniment for a young, up-and-coming singer. The first track they record is 'Out of This World' but the lyrics are unconvincing and the whole thing comes out sounding awkward and odd. It wouldn't be wronging anybody involved too heinously to suggest that these aren't the purest expressions of Bill's art ever lathe-cut into posterity.

On 8 December, he is in the studio again but with Paul Motian this time. They play together for the first time in six months. It is good to see him. He still has the moustache he was sporting in June and when he smiles he is genial and sharp-looking, like a businessman unable to take his money-making game too seriously. They don't dwell on the recent past but shake hands warmly and put arms around each other. They are glad that the album has been well received and that people are giving Scotty . . . well, as close to his due as he's likely to get any more.

As they stand around between takes or wait for technical adjustments, voices pipe up to sing the record's praises. It has that beautiful feel, they say, like you're there in the room, in the front row, and before long there is an entire small gathering chirping its appreciation. The audience's intervention gives it that human touch, they say, the real world, strangely, making the whole thing seem *other*worldly . . . Bill implies his thanks with a nod of his head.

They ask him if he's seen *DownBeat* – and they're all speaking quite loud suddenly, as though that were the only way of getting through to him. The annual readers' poll has him in third place, behind Oscar Peterson and Monk, and another chorus of congratulation ensues.

§

Bill is more or less operational – and traceable – again. Which ought to be sufficient for some of the fainter outlines to be inked in or filled out. Yet the pallor of biography remains. It seems almost redundant, for example, to say that his memories of the Sunday he played at the Village Vanguard, with friends, have begun to pale or that his reaction to the record itself has taken on some of the black and white distance of its cover imagery. Such a reflection is no less true of anybody who ever had cause to remember an event or encounter with affection or regret. Not that Bill will purposely sit down to listen to his own records anyway – he has that much in common with the jazzer breed. Always the next gig, the next collaboration, the next expression of their practicable art. So whatever remains of that Sunday, its purest expression is less that which was captured on the recording than the transference it achieves beyond the medium. For the improvising musician, and perhaps for Bill in particular, it is less about the fear of nothing being good enough to look back on than about the fact of that music no longer being played. And this is the gap that memory – and the memory of music quite specifically – bridges; it arcs into a private sphere where ordinary centrifuges have no pull. A song lasts for four minutes forty-eight seconds, but while you can live it again, in the other place . . .

Inasmuch as it has to do with Bill directly, then, and whatever rehabilitation he was able to manage in the nineteen summers he lived after 1961 – years in which he experienced the further losses of his parents (Harry first, then Mary) made appearances on the Johnny Carson show, and received awards and accolades and news of his brother's suicide – the fundamental question is one of life, of how to live, precisely, in music. The certain song, the harmony or progression or the sounding out of something unresolved that reminds you in vital, dominant tones of how much you love. It feels like salvation. Only that the emotion prefigures something else too – they have the exact same source – namely the tears to be shed in the death of that love. You feel at once buoyant and bereft, and attachment, to a person let's say, becomes perilously fragile. And you may wish, just then, for the loved one to reveal themselves, in all their earthly glory – a sort of instinctive turning away from the miracle. But while you *are* able to bear the weight, which is to say, of course, the weightlessness, it is, surely, the most irrefutable proof – and the most wonderful possibility – of life.

§

Paul, it transpires, is keen to start working again after their December recording date. He is Motian by name and desire if not always by pronunciation. They are in touch with another young bassist, who goes by the name of Chuck, and the challenge to the two survivors of the previous trio, which they feel in shared looks and the things they refrain from saying, is not to think of him as the new Scott. But Chuck, as might be said to befit *his* name, has confidence and vigour in prodigious plenty, not to mention technique and good sense, and it is hard.

Chuck is in on the December recording too. They don't

quite gel, which is only to be expected, perhaps – and they've been hired, besides, as a straight-ahead, albeit uncommonly talented, rhythm section. There must be enough there to suggest interesting developments to come, though, because, shortly after, they go to Syracuse together, in upstate New York, where they have a few gigs planned and where, with a bit of luck, they'll be able to bed in properly.

The drive up is on a bright winter's day. It is just about pleasant in the sunlight but cutting cold in the shadows. When they catch glimpses of the Hudson, it looks as if it has been covered over with a thin, reflective film, like ice in formation, and that the water is flowing under the surface only. Then they are on the interstate and counting down the miles in pleasant camaraderie.

They chat about the business of jazz – who's working with whom, who's playing where and who's paying. The safe banter of working musicians. Bill doesn't say all that much but is glad to have the chatter about him and to feel in his cheeks a flush of uncomplicated existence. They stop at a roadside diner for burgers and coffee and look on with lazy amusement as Paul flirts with the waitress.

When they get going again, the road ahead feels longer than ever and the chat dries up pretty quickly. The two older men nod off, Bill in the front passenger seat, Paul stretched out in the back, leaving Chuck to keep himself awake at the wheel.

When Bill comes to, they are no more than half an hour from their destination. But the nap has only served to accentuate his tiredness and brings with it the old nagging, which he registers this time in his legs and in his teeth too. He tries all manner of postures and positions in his seat but can't shake it – licking his lips, rubbing his jaw with both hands. He tries to combat it after that with what he can notice through the windscreen.

Up ahead, a road sign comes into view and Bill knows at once that it will have significance. They are coming up to the Cherry Valley Turnpike and – true enough – the sign points to Lafayette and Route 20. Which means that to their left, beyond the little village of Cardiff and the middling towns of Auburn, Seneca Falls and Waterloo, is Geneva and the homecoming Scotty never made it to. Bill finds himself hoping that there is still a place laid for him at the kitchen table. The road sign rushes up on them and he stares at it intently. It is gone in a flash but, for some time after, his eyes remain at the point where it moved out of his vision. Fifty yards, a hundred back already, the forking off of him and me and I and you.

I am happy to acknowledge here a Creative Wales Award from the Arts Council of Wales which enabled me to begin work in earnest on this book. Likewise Peter Pettinger's *How My Heart Sings* which, alongside other material both online and in print, was a plentiful source of musical and biographical detail. I am grateful also to Eliot Zigmund for sharing with me some of his experiences playing with the Bill Evans Trio.

For their advice, support and all-round excellence, I would like to thank Jason Arthur, Tom Avery, Hélène Bouillon, Jon Gower, Gwydion Gruffudd, Lucy Luck, Bambos Neophytou and Catrin Wright. *Diolch o galon.*